THE ALLIGATOR REPORT

Stories by W. P. Kinsella

A TOTEM BOOK
Toronto

First published 1985
by Coffee House Press
This edition published 1986
by TOTEM BOOKS
a division of Collins Publishers
100 Lesmill Road, Don Mills, Ontario
© 1985 by W.P. Kinsella

Drawings by Gaylord Schanilec

Some of these stories first appeared in the following magazines: Blue
Buffalo; Canadian Short Story Magazine; Cross Canada Writers' Quar-
terly; Ethos; Iowa City Creative Reading Series Magazine; Karake;
Martlet Magazine; Only Paper Today; Out of the Blue; Raincoast Chroni-
cles; Simcoe Review; Waves; Wee Giant; and Whetstone. "Gabon"
appeared in the USA in North American Review, and in Canada, under
the title "I Pay My Rent," it appeared in Dandelion Magazine and Best
Canadian Stories: 1985.

Canadian Cataloguing in Publication Data

Kinsella, W.P.
    The alligator report: stories

ISBN 0-00-223170-0

I. Title.

PS8571.I57A82 1987   C813'.54   C86-094974-5
PR9199.3.K59A74 1987

Designed by Allan Kornblum

Printed and bound in the United States of America

CONTENTS

INTRODUCTION

Three days after I signed the contract for this book Richard Brautigan's death was announced. I can't think of another writer who has influenced my life and career as much. If I could own only one book it would be Brautigan's mysterious parable *In Watermelon Sugar*. I think *Dreaming of Babylon* is the funniest novel I have ever read.

Many of the short, surreal pieces in this book owe a debt to Richard Brautigan. I publicly call these vignettes *Brautigans* and many have been published in groups of three or four as such. Brautigan's delicate, visual, whimsical, facetious writing appealed to a whole generation of us who were able to identify with the gentle, loving losers of his stories. He and director Robert Altman are the two famous people I would most like to shake hands with. Richard Brautigan was an extremely private person, one who apparently was unable to take joy from his accomplishments, but concentrated instead upon what he had not done or felt he was no longer able to do. A few years ago a friend and I decided to phone Richard Brautigan, an uncharacteristic gesture, for I too am a very private person. Unfortunately his home near Livingston, Montana had a silent listing.

The letter which follows I wrote to Richard Brautigan in 1980. Though he must have received thousands like it, I'm glad I wrote, I'm glad I let him know how he touched my life. I'm only sorry that it wasn't enough, that I couldn't have done more.

December, 1980

Dear Richard Brautigan:

I am just now reading *The Tokyo-Montana Express,* reading it slowly, a page or two at a time, like trying to make Christmas candy last until Easter. It is very hard to write a fan letter, for what do you say after you say, "I admire your books very much. They bring me a great deal of pleasure. I wish I could write like you." I don't know. I do write. In fact I am quite a well-known writer in Canada. But I am not very well known in the United States, except in Iowa, where I once brought a dead baseball player back to life. They buy my books there because one of them has 'Iowa' in the title. I think I should have put 'Iowa' in the title of all my books; there are four of them at the moment.

I have just read a story in your book where you talk about driving to Bozeman. I once drove from Edmonton to Bozeman in the dead of winter in a lumbering metallic-blue DeSoto that was old enough to be my father. I drove there to compete in a public speaking contest against people from Montana, Idaho, and British Columbia. Bozeman claimed to be the Convention Capital of Montana. The hotel was dark and poorly heated. Each bar that I visited had a few sodden cowboys in sheepskin-lined mackinaws, but no unattached women, which was what I was looking for.

The judges were all Montana men with square jaws and western suits. I gave a rousing speech, easily the best in my class but because I critizized Robert Welch and the John Birch Society, I did not even place. I learned that Montana men have nothing to do in the wintertime but impregnate their wives and look at the horizon waiting for the Red Tide they know is sweeping toward them across the frozen land.

I also teach writing, whatever that means. Many of my students have published, but I wonder if they would have eventually even if our paths had not crossed.

I have just written a novel about a man who drives from Iowa to New Hampshire, kidnaps J. D. Salinger and takes him to a baseball game at Fenway Park. Somehow it loses something being summarized like that. Perhaps I will write a novel about a man who kidnaps Richard Brautigan and keeps him locked in his rumpus room which has a trout stream and paper-mache model of Mt. Fujiyama. He makes you write a "Brauti-gan" every day, like laying a golden egg, and rushes out to his bookie and bets the Brautigan on a very slow horse running in the seventh race at Aqueduct. Then again I may not.

I suppose what I'm trying to say in a roundabout way is thank you for writing what you have written. I'll close with a quote from a fan letter I received from an editor in Boston after he read my story about the dead baseball player. But if it is the way he feels about my work, it is also the way I feel about yours:

> " You do something in your stories that few writers do well—especially today—and that is to make the reader *love* your characters. They exude a warm glow. They are so real, so vulnerable, so good, that they remind us of that side of human nature which makes living and loving and striving after dreams worth the effort. I, for one, came away with a delicious smile on my face and a soft little tear in my eye—and I felt pretty damn good about being alive for the rest of the day."

Very best regards,

Bill Kinsella

Dedication:

In memory of Richard Brautigan
1935–1984

Part One

Vancouver

THE POST OFFICE OCTOPUS

I can never remember the name of the street where I live, which makes it difficult for me to give my address to the public library or the immigration authorities, not that either of them have ever asked for it.

I reside in what can be best described as a rather bohemian two-room suite on the second floor of a very old house with white siding, which looks out on the grounds of a none-too-affluent private school in East Vancouver, where girls in blue-and-white uniforms play grass hockey on fall afternoons. I have a large brass bed with a black teak headboard on which tiers of toga-wrapped figures are carved. The bed has not been made for several years. I also own an antique oak table with a number of paint stains on it: a reminder that I once shared the apartment with a Czech art student named Zonia, who had massive dark eyes, big and black as greatcoat buttons.

The front hall of the house is very dark. The baseboards are varnished, as are the stairs, railings, and trim around the door. At the base of the banister is a varnished ball about the size of a melon. Someone has glued a sun-yellow happy face on it.

Inside the front door, to the right, is a bracketed shelf attached to the wall, with five mailboxes underneath, as well as a small, dark table covered with a linen runner which has the embroidered face of a cat on it. The other tenants in the house change with alarming frequency. The shelf and table are always covered with unclaimed mail.

Unclaimed letters depress me. I wonder how people can disappear from the face of the earth, leaving behind them a flock of unclaimed mail, fluttering like doves in confusion.

I have it on good authority that the Post Office has an octopus who reads the unclaimed mail, looking for checks, money orders, and cash, all the time hoping for crab. Though he has never found one, he never gives up hoping that someday someone will mail a small, delicious crab to a friend who has moved and that the crab will wind up in the dead letter office. The octopus reads very quickly, his eight tentacles whirling like a pinwheel. The reading is done in an apple-green room with a twelve-foot-long fluorescent light fixture. Sometimes when he is reading very fast, just the hint of a giggle comes from the bins of homeless letters, for occasionally, like a group of orphans seated in front of a clown, they forget that no one really wants them.

Several years ago my ex-wife sent me a very important-looking registered letter with a lot of stamps on it. It annoyed me to think that she knew my address and I didn't. I threw the letter out on the porch where it lay in the rain for several days until it swelled up like a frog. I then wrote DECEASED across the envelope and drew an ornate arrow pointing to the return address. I distinctly heard the bloated letter croak as I slipped it into a mailbox.

THE VANCOUVER CHAPTER OF THE HOWARD G. SCHARFF MEMORIAL SOCIETY

Among a tangle of rooming houses on Cordova Street is one with the unlikely name of Minnesota Rooms. On the second floor, a Chinese opened a slot in a dark door labeled OFFICE, took my two dollars and proffered a key attached to a rectangular piece of cardboard on which the number eight was heavily pencilled.

The hooker accompanying me had short, plum-colored hair and green eyes. Clutching the key I followed her up some steep stairs to a tiny room on the third floor. She wore tight, faded blue jeans and a low-cut white blouse with no bra. She appeared nervous as a cat until we reached the room, then, like a fighter who is only at home in the ring, she took complete charge. She carried on a running monologue as she sat her large leather handbag on the dresser, hung the white sweater she carried over her arm on the back of the room's only chair, and butted her cigarette in a chipped glass ashtray.

"You can get undressed," she said, looking at me where I stood awkwardly just inside the door. She stepped past me and opened the door I had just closed. "Nature calls," she said, and smiling, added, "You don't have to pay me until I come back. I'm no rip-off artist."

While she was gone I discovered something I'm sure no

one else in the world knows. The single bed, with its prison-bar head and base covered in chipped brown enamel, was manufactured by the Howard G. Scharff Corporation, of Baltimore, Maryland. By the age and condition of the bed, Howard G. Scharff must be dead these many years. But, how marvellous to have little monuments to your memory in all the two-dollar short-time rooms, in all the creaking hotels, of all the skid rows of America. I would like to be remembered the same way.

GABON

I have lived in this massive, old frame house for four years. Only Gabon has been here longer. The house leans at odd, erotic angles. I'm still not sure that I've been in all the rooms and apartments. Multiple additions have been built on over the many years since the house was new. Some owner, desperate for money, rented a sun porch or pantry, and built on a new sun porch or pantry, which was later rented out by a subsequent owner. Years ago, the double garage was converted into an apartment. Later, a room was added on top of the garage, then still another room was piled on top of that.

A Mrs. Kryzanowski owns the property now, inherited from her husband, a hollow-cheeked, cancerous-looking man who cashed in his pale soul soon after I arrived. He had purchased the house from the estate of an elderly Chinese, who had died in one of the sun porches amid stacks of Chinese newspapers and three bamboo cages filled with thimble-sized canaries.

Before the Chinese, history blurs.

Gabon lives in the attic above the third floor. He occupies a tiny loft with one dark, triangular window that overlooks the back alley. The attic is reached by pulling down a metal ladder, which hugs the ceiling like a long, wrought-iron spider, and climbing through a trap door.

I'm sure Gabon's presence in the attic must violate thousands of fire and building code regulations, but none of us are about to call in outsiders, who, in order to *protect* us, would evict us. The rent is cheap; the house is warm; and each of us lives with our own secrets, which may be as frayed as a favorite blanket or as vicious as a Tasmanian devil.

Gabon is small and brown with bird-like ankles and wrists; his nose is hooked, and black tufts of hair bristle from his head at odd angles. I knew someone from Sumatra who looked like him: tiny, starved-looking, cinnamon-skinned. There is a sour, bachelor smell about Gabon, of emptied ashtrays and soiled clothing.

Whenever I meet him on the sidewalk or in the halls, he nods shyly. "I pay my rent," he informs me, speaking in a sibilant whisper, his accent unidentifiable: Spanish? Greek? Arabic of some ilk? I suspect he knows only two English phrases: "Nice day," offered even when it is raining torrentially, and "I pay my rent." The latter is delivered as if he is asking a question like, "How are you?"

The phrase must have impressed Mrs. Kryzanowski, for when I say, after counting twenty-dollar bills into her blueish hand, "Tell me about Gabon," she replies, "He pays his rent." The expression on her pink, naugahyde face lets me know unequivocally that Gabon is a good tenant, and that she would be happier if I paid my rent on time more often and asked fewer questions.

"I pay my rent too," I say, trying to smile disarmingly.

"Sometimes," says Mrs. Krysanowski.

But I refuse to be dismissed so easily. I stand leaning on the doorjamb, waiting. Mrs. Kryzanowski is wearing a ghastly, flowered housecoat; her white hair has incongruous lemon streaks in it and is wound around candy-apple-blue rollers. Her face is paved with makeup that may well have been applied with a palette knife.

"Noisy, noisy," she finally says. "A jockey. Broked his neck once," and she makes a cracking motion with her large hands, like snapping invisible kindling.

"Noisy?" I say.

"Walk, walk, walk. Ax-ersize maybe? Who knows. Everybody's crazy over there."

Mrs. Kryzanowski lives two blocks away in a one-story, basementless house with unlevel floors covered with bulging linoleum. She never visits the "Castle," as our rooming house is referred to by residents and neighbors alike.

"He has a *doght*," she volunteers, smiling conspiratorially. "He tinks I don't know."

Mrs. Kryzanowski obviously has a spy at the Castle. It is probably Grabarkewitcz, who lives in a room below me in the company of a magical cat. Mrs. Kryzanowski had Grabarkewitcz's room painted last month, the only maintenance she has authorized since she has owned the Castle.

A dog. Interesting.

Night and day I haunt the halls of the Castle, inhaling the odors of varnish, cooked cabbage, mothballs, and dust. Mrs. Kryzanowski harbors quite a genteel collection of loners and losers. Tenants who disturb the status quo are dealt with swiftly. Last summer, a stringy-haired thug rented a first-floor room and soon had it swarming with beer-swilling friends who argued, fought, played a tinny radio at full volume, and urinated out the window into Mrs. Kryzanowski's caragana hedge.

One afternoon, a lithe Oriental with steel-colored hair

and bitter eyes called on the thug and his friends. The caller was verbally abused and threatened. The young Oriental bowed curtly as the door was slammed in his face.

The next time the thug exited by the side door, there was one sharp bleat of pain, brief scuffling in the caragana, then silence. Late that evening, the thug moved out, his thug friends carrying his few possessions. The thug carried only a few soiled clothes crushed to his body with his left arm. His right arm bore a blazing white cast, resting like an angel in a clean, white sling.

I knew how Gabon reached his living quarters, but had never seen the deed accomplished. Like most of us here, Gabon had no employment and kept irregular hours. I lurked behind my curtains for two days before I spied Gabon approaching the house. I huffed up two flights of stairs and down a long corridor. I was loitering beneath the black ladder when Gabon arrived.

"Evening," I said.

"Nice day," said Gabon. He was clutching an apple in his right hand.

"It is," I said. It was.

"I pay my rent," said Gabon, again treating the statement as a question. Perhaps he had been misled by a deceitful English-as-a-second-language instructor.

Gabon nervously forced the apple into a side pocket, then flexing his knees, sprang straight into the air and grabbed the bottom rung of the ladder with both hands. There was barely enough of Gabon—ninety pounds would be my guess—to pull the ladder down until the bottom rung was a foot from the floor. When the ladder was in position, he quickly scampered up the eight or so

rungs, like a native scaling a palm tree, and pushed open
the trap door to the attic. He disappeared like a burglar
and the ladder swung eerily back into place, emitting a
few soft, metal groans.

I remained in the dim hall for a long time. Gabon did
pace about a great deal, sometimes seeming to break into a
run. He also seemed to be talking to someone, though the
words were indistinguishable, and could have come from
a radio.

He must have been uneasy about his encounter with
me, for, after about twenty minutes, the trap door
creaked open and Gabon hung his head down and peered
furtively around. I was pressed against the wall at the head
of the stairs out of view.

Back in my room, I opened the window and crawled
out onto the porch roof below me and crawled about
twenty feet. I carefully stood up next to an addition to the
Castle at shoulder height. By pulling myself up and over
two more portions of the building, and risking great em-
barrassment and multiple fractures, I was able to climb
onto the roof of Gabon's loft. I slithered forward to the
very peak of the roof and, by hanging precariously over
the edge, was able to peer into Gabon's triangular window. It was a crisp October night and I was silvered by
the moon as I hung grotesquely, like a broken TV antenna.

In the loft, which was lit by the yellowish light from
one sixty-watt bulb, sat Gabon, not on a chair or bed, but
on the back of a small, shaggy, brown-and-white pony.

Gabon, no larger than a ten-year-old, was dressed in
jockey silks of parrot-green and ivory, a white-and-green
jockey's cap on his head, goggles resting on the crown of
the cap.

The pony was a bit over three feet tall. Gabon sat on a scaled-down racing saddle, it and his tall boots polished to the color of gleaming liver.

In one corner of the loft was Gabon's pallet. In the other, cordoned off by small packing crates, was straw for bedding and grass for eating. Gabon rode the pony in a slow circle; the middle of the room was covered with brown indoor-outdoor carpet. The pony pranced. Gabon waved to the crowd.

I tried to imagine Gabon smuggling the pony into the loft. It was too big to remove now, but I suppose as a colt it would have been no larger than a full-grown spaniel.

On a brilliant October night, in one of the loneliest places on earth, Gabon paraded around the winner's circle under the blazing sun of Hialeah, Pimlico, or Churchill Downs, accepting the accolades, remembering the clash of the starting gate, the yelp of the crowd as his horse lunged forward—sleek, powerful, pliant as butter between his thighs.

SYZYGY

In the downstairs suite lives a young man named Grabarkewitcz. I know his name because it is on his mailbox,
punched out on a narrow strip of coffee-colored tape
which stretches across the stovepipe-black surface. The
mailboxes sit in a black row like so many traumatized
crows. The remarkable thing about Grabarkewitcz is that
he has a bathroom of his own. Upstairs, I have to share a
bathroom at the end of the hall with whatever itinerant
happens to be squatting in the suite next to mine. At the
moment there resides therein an unemployed Serbian juggler, his aged mother, and a woman who may be wife, sis-
ter, lover, hanger-on, or all of the above. They have been
placed there by the Welfare. It is not easy to find a job for a
juggling Serb. The three of them spend their days staring
out the window at the slushy street and grit-encrusted
sidewalk waiting for a circus parade to pass the house, led
by a clown dressed in buttercup yellow, cartwheeling and
displaying a sign reading JUGGLER WANTED.

Occasionally, Grabarkewitcz invites me into his apartment for coffee. We are both lonely; he not so much as I
because he has a cat for company, a large, square-jawed
tabby with emerald eyes. He addresses the cat by an un-
pronounceable name, which to me sounds like Syzygy.
Perhaps it means Kitty in some ephemeral European dia-
lect.

Kitty sleeps in the bathroom sink. The first time I

walked into the bathroom I thought the sink was full of fur coat, that perhaps Grabarkewitcz took in fur coats to launder in order to supplement his income—I have never asked Grabarkewitcz what he does for a living. Then the cat moved slightly, twitched as it swatted down a sparrow in its dreams; it filled the sink level until it appeared to be full of tabby-cat water. When Kitty moved the water rippled but nothing slopped on the floor.

One day when I stopped by Grabarkewitcz was shaving. I stood in the doorway and watched him shave his long, blue-stubbled face and neck. The sink was full of cat. The water easily drained through the fur. Grabarkewitcz flicked his razor and lather and whiskers splattered on the cat. The stream of water from the tap washed them away.

"I think your cat is dead," I said to Grabarkewitcz.

"Here, Syzygy," said Grabarkewitcz in reply.

The cat did not respond, but the tabby stripes began to swirl around the sink forming a tabby whirlpool which eventually exited down the drain leaving only a few hairs and a few flecks of shaving lather on the sides of the bowl.

"Cats are independent devils," said Grabarkewitcz. "They never come when you call them."

THE SECRET

On a wet Vancouver afternoon, with rain tapping clandestinely against the brittle panes of my lone window, Grabarkewitcz tells me his secret. I am propped on my bed, my weak pillow doubled behind my head. Grabarkewitcz sits on the room's only chair, rubbing his long blue-stubbled face and neck. Grabarkewitcz occupies a suite on the ground floor of this decaying rooming house in East Vancouver. He shifts his long, pointed feet, which are encased in unshined black dress shoes, and in answer to a question about his past, begins to speak.

"I am a convicted felon," Grabarkewitcz begins, hunching forward, his hand on his unshaven chin making a crunching sound.

Felon is an odd word, I think. I have always associated it with those pale, moldy-smelling wedges of fruit one finds on second-rate buffet tables. I sniff. Grabarkewitcz smells of stale rooms and welfare.

"There is a little-known statute in B.C. which prohibits carnal and salacious activities with books. I was convicted of Second Degree Bookfondling," he says to the floor, then adds quickly "I hope this won't affect our friendship."

"Of course not," I say. "Why should your literary preferences affect our relationship?"

"I was born with the desire," Grabarkewitcz goes on. "I wasn't corrupted by an older bookfondler as society often supposes. As a child, while my friends were sneaking into their mothers' bedrooms, dressing in their negligees and garter-belts, I would scatter my mother's Harlequin Romances across her silk bedspread and fondle the book jackets." Grabarkewitcz stares up at me, his dark eyes full of pain.

"I tried to live a normal life," he goes on. "For years I was a closet fondler. I frequented dark areas in library stacks, special collection rooms, empty aisles in second-hand bookstores. I married, fathered two beautiful daughters. I should have moved to a province where the law doesn't persecute bookfondlers.

"Eventually my darker desires overcame my good sense. I would buy hardcover books, novels, coffee-table books, nonfiction, even children's books. I'd take them to a secluded spot, remove their dustjackets, and photograph them nude.

"I hid the photographs in a shoe-box in the top of my closet. That was my undoing. My wife found the photos; they broke her heart. Of course, she left me, but before she did she called the police.

"Second Degree Bookfondling carries a penalty of fourteen years to life. One of the provisions of the divorce decree was that I not even be allowed to know the whereabouts of my wife and children.

"When I was released, after years in a segregated area of the prison, the John Howard Society found me this suite, arranged for welfare. There are few job opportunities for convicted bookfondlers."

"I sympathize," I said.

"You don't believe me," accused Grabarkewitcz, shifting his feet, rubbing his bristly cheek.

"I believe you," I said.

"I only photograph my cat these days," said Grabarke-witcz. "Nothing kinky, though I sometimes dress him in doll's clothes."

The rain drizzled against the window.

THE SILVER PORCUPINE

From my window I watch the rain on the street, Vancouver rain, heavy as long silver drills: feeble little jackhammers which try in their own way to turn the streets and sidewalks to rubble. The gutters swell like bloated fish, appropriate a colored reflection, carry it along a curb and into an open grate. In the sewers of Vancouver swirl a kaleidoscope of reflections, fighting against the stream, breaking up into pinpoints of exotic light, like many tiny and fragile fish.

When the wind blows high, raindrops imbed themselves in the skin, like needles or porcupine quills tattooing stories of the street on an unprotected arm, or a half-turned face. When I was young I lived in a prairie city, cold as a freezer. My family owned an ancient record player and cabinet, tall as a refrigerator, square and rigid, smelling of furniture polish and dusty velvet. The lid over the record player opened upward and was propped open with a small stick, like an animal trap. On the inside of the lid was a colored decal, a picture of the hopeful dog staring in awe at the trumpet-shaped speaker which dispensed his master's voice.

In either corner of the record player just out of reach of the turntable, like tiny silver chamber pots, submerged to their top edges, were the needle holders. The needles were about the size of porcupine quills, but bright as chrome. Each needle was good for only a few dozen plays. The new needles were kept in the right-hand receptacle, the used ones in the left. The used needles were retained because when the supply of new needles ran out, the least damaged used ones were pressed into service.

I liked to stir the bowls of needles with an index finger, making them careen round the shiny bowl like miniature fish being chased, the odd one riding high on the bowl rim like a motorcycle daredevil I had seen at a fair.

Tonight, in this rooming house in Vancouver, a thousand miles and nearly as many years from the cold prairie and my past, I heard a silver porcupine tick across the front porch and snuffle at the door. And I could imagine yellow tines of streetlight shattering against his quills, bursting like fireworks in the rain.

Part Two

Books by the Pound

BOOKS BY THE POUND

The sign in the window of the used bookstore read "Books by the Pound." The proprietor was small and wizened and had hair the color of an old dog. On his counter was an equally old Toledo Scale, with "Honest Weight" stencilled in curly golden letters across the face of the large white cylinder, which showed the weight bobbing back and forth like the bubble in a carpenter's level. The scale was the type that still graces the counters of dark, coffee-smelling general stores in failing hamlets all across America.

There was a special on the day I was there. All books by Ernest Hemingway were sixty cents a pound, marked down from eighty-five cents. *The Snows of Kilimanjaro and Other Stories* cost me twenty cents, a terrific bargain.

"That's a terrific bargain," I said to the old man, whose eyes were the same creamy yellow as his hair. "You're selling your produce too cheaply," I went on. "For a book like this, you should charge for the weight inside, not just for the weight of the paper. Think of it . . . Harry dying of gangrene at the base of Kilimanjaro, Nick Adams in all his incarnations, Ole Andreson, Jack Brennan, Soldier Bartlett, Francis Macomber, his wife, Wilson the big-game hunter, and . . ."

"That's a weird idea you've got there, son," the proprietor said.

"You could charge for the okapis and gazelles," I rattled

on, "water buffalo, lions, the fish and the rhinos, the giraffes, and the buzzards with crimson wattles that always sit, waiting for death to pay its call. In Hemingway, death always has a finger on the scale, so to speak. There are shadows of buzzards in every one of his stories." I was suddenly struck by an idea. "How much do you figure a buzzard weighs?" I asked.

"I don't know," said the old man.

"Twenty pounds," I said. "Does that sound fair?"

"If you say so."

"You could sell buzzard for ten cents a pound. That would come to two dollars a buzzard. Then you could advertise a book like this," I was still waving *The Snows of Kilimanjaro,* "as being on sale for half a buzzard. That would be a dollar. You sold it to me for twenty cents. I've just increased your volume five-fold."

"You have a good head for business," the old man said.

"You have to think of things like that," I said. "Think of the weight inside this book. Think of the war stories, all that equipment: tanks, trucks, shells, bullets. How much do you suppose a tank weighs?"

"My books wouldn't stand that kind of mark-up," said the proprietor, smiling just a little with his eyes, like an old dog would smile.

"You're right," I said. I went on to buy forty cents worth of Flannery O'Connor and four ounces of a writer with my last name, who turned out to be a priest and a bad writer. I put another book on the scale and stood staring down at the registered weight where it glided back and forth like a car rocking in a snowdrift. We both gazed at the weight as if I were purchasing precious stones at a diamond wholesale, or pork tenderloin at an old-fashioned butcher shop.

"You should consider my suggestion," I said.

"I don't think so," said the old man, giving me another old-dog smile, "I used up all my imagination deciding to sell books by the pound."

THE EAST END
UMBRELLA COMPANY
ENDOWMENT
FOR THE ARTS

In Vancouver, in the '60s, when five dollars still bought groceries for one for a week, on one of the decaying side streets stood a tall, elderly, frame house. At first glance it appeared to be vacant, for no curtains or blinds showed in the windows. Far in the past the house had been painted an off-shade of cream, with chocolate-brown trim; the cream-colored paint weathered to a buckskin color, flagrantly peeling until the exterior looked as though it had several hundred leaves glued to it. On the left, the house scrunched tightly against the corrugated fence of a scrap iron dealership; behind the silver fence lay an endless array of rusted girders, engine blocks, and uniquely shaped but unidentifiable metal objects, displayed in a casual, almost erotic tangle.

There was a small sign just above the shabby front door: spindly brown lettering on a white background read East End Umbrella Co. On the right side of the property, crossing from the corner of the house to the property line, then to the back of the lot, was an unpainted, but still honey-colored, eight-foot, pin-board fence. I passed the East End Umbrella Co. each time I walked to Gas Town, or down to the strip of aging hotels on East Hastings Street.

Once, as I walked home late at night, I noticed a light in the front window of East End Umbrella. The light disappointed me, for it destroyed my fantasy of the house being vacant; I imagined the house cold and musty, unoccupied except for mice and a skeletal umbrella or two. Because of the height of the windows I could see nothing, even when I stopped on the sidewalk and stood on tiptoe, except a single bulb on a cord, dangling like a lollipop, and the top corner of an old-fashioned wooden filing cabinet.

A few days later, in the afternoon, my illusions about the East End Umbrella Co. were further diminished. As I approached the house, the front door opened and a very elderly Oriental emerged. He hobbled down the narrow front steps and gingerly picked his way toward Chinatown. His hair was slush-gray, his cheeks hollow; he wore a loose-fitting black tunic and black slippers, both of which may well have been made from umbrella silk. He carried a rolled black umbrella with a silver point. He leaned heavily on the umbrella as if it were a cane. His breath whistled sharply as we passed and he smelled of mysterious herbs.

Somehow I had hoped to learn, by staring at the house, by observing the old gentleman, something about the manufacture of umbrellas. Am I the only person who ponders the mystery of umbrella manufacture? I have often wondered how the thin metal ribs, fragile as bird bones, stand up to the pressure from the taut fabric. How can those same little ribs fold and unfold again and again? How is the strange release mechanism installed in the handle? Are umbrellas now manufactured by computer? Is there a machine where fabric and metal are fed into one end, and where finished umbrellas are spit out a slot at the other?

The second half of this story has to do with a man named Bulgar. I occasionally stopped in at the Sunshine Hotel, or at one of the other teeming bars along East Hastings Street, to enjoy a few beers and soak up the sights and sounds, immersing myself in the beehive-like atmosphere for an hour or two.

A familiar face at the Sunshine was Bulgar, a lumberjack, or at least he looked like a lumberjack. His scarred, hairy hands dwarfed his beer glass; he wore a green-checkered mackinaw, khaki work pants, and heavy construction boots. His spiky hair was wild and untrimmed.

Bulgar usually drank alone at a table just inside the Hastings Street entrance to the Sunshine. However, occasionally he fastened his eyes on someone sitting nearby, motioned them toward his table, usually by waving a crumpled dollar bill, and in a voice which sounded as if he had a pound of rock chips in his throat, said loudly, "Bulgar! Drink!"

Most everyone in the Sunshine was short of money so Bulgar's invitation was seldom refused. He beckoned me to his table on two occasions. Each time he bought me a glass of beer, and silently observed me, head cocked, eyes slightly crossed, as I silently drank. My attempts at conversation were ignored. When I thanked him he bobbed his head several times and repeated his name.

Bulgar, if that was indeed his name, was about forty, with high, Slavic cheekbones, a red face, a long thin nose. He had a trenchlike cleft in his chin.

Late one evening I left the Sunshine and, walking in a light drizzle in the direction of Cordova Street, I heard

pounding footsteps on the pavement behind me. I turned
to see Bulgar slogging toward me.

"Wait up!" he shouted.

When he caught up with me he announced, "We walk!" I felt uneasy. I had never seen Bulgar outside the hotel. And although I had never known him to be violent, violence was a way of life at the Sunshine, and its denizens were not exactly known for their acts of compassion.

Bulgar towered over me. He was smiling, but his eyes, which were always just a little out of focus, were too bright; they glittered like chrome each time we passed beneath a streetlight.

He walked beside me with long, determined strides, as if he were marching in a foreign army. As we approached the East End Umbrella Co. he slowed, and turned up the driveway. He stopped in front of the gate and lifted the silver latch. I remained on the side, slightly alarmed at what he was doing, wanting no part of a spur-of-the-moment B & E.

"Bulgar," my mackinawed acquaintance whispered loudly, as he beckoned me to follow him. I approached until I stood with one hand resting on the damp, honey-colored gatepost. Inside, the yard was landscaped, the grass neatly cut. A few leafless, waist-high cherry trees looked like brown dancers atwirl. The rear cross-fence ran parallel to the back of the house, where some ragged stairs emerged from a glassed-in porch.

A few feet in front of those steps, on the lawn just to the right of the thin sidewalk, lay an umbrella, unfurled, the convex outer survace facing toward us. Bulgar advanced to a point three feet or so in front of the open umbrella. Although his back was toward me it was not difficult for me to comprehend what he was about to do. Men have a universal set of movements when they are unzipping their pants and extracting their penis. Bulgar proceeded to urinate on the umbrella, for a long time; his bladder must have had the capacity of a car radiator. I pictured Bulgar with a honeycomblike radiator running chest to crotch under his mackinaw.

The urine splattered off the umbrella making a tzzzz sound as Bulgar directed the stream to test as much of the taut, silken surface as possible. Tiny tentacles of steam rose in the damp, after-midnight air. When he finished Bulgar sighed, zipped himself up, then turned toward the nearest cherry tree which was some five feet to his right. He bent and felt around the base of the tree with his huge fingers and came up holding an envelope of some kind.

As he returned to where I was standing by the gate I saw he was clutching a plastic sandwich bag. He opened the flap and extracted a five dollar bill.

"Bulgar," he said, smiling through splayed teeth. He nodded toward the umbrella, indicating it to be my turn.

"No thank you," I said.

Bulgar shrugged. As he closed the gate he waved, a movement somewhere between a farewll gesture and a salute. As he did I thought I caught a flash of movement behind the portion of glassed-in porch still visible from outside the fence.

Bulgar again took pains to show me the sleek five dollar bill before he stuffed it into his back pocket. We walked on in silence. When we reached Gore Street I indicated my need to change direction.

"Bulgar," said Bulgar.

"Goodnight," I said.

Streetlights reflected dully off the wet pavement.

What had I just witnessed? Was Bulgar doing some sort of consumer testing for East End Umbrella?

A five dollar bill in a baggie. Intriguing.

Was there really a sallow, oriental face at the sun porch window?

I walked on slowly down the silent, misty streets of East Vancouver. I considered returning, lifting the silver gate-latch. Would there be a second umbrella spread and waiting? Would there be a second envelope beneath a second twirling cherry tree? Slowly, I began to retrace my steps. I speeded up; I could already feel the dry, crisp five dollar bill warming in my shirt pocket.

A PAGE FROM
THE MARRIAGE MANUAL
FOR SONGHEES BRIDES

I carried them in my taxi several times, an Indian couple about 40 and 35. It is not really my taxi but I consider it mine while I am driving it. It belongs to a Lithuanian with a gold tooth who wears a shiny serge suit and a vest with potatoes for buttons.

She was huge, covered in a number of layers of soft fat. Her eyes didn't like her very much, and like animals on the edge of a forest retreated back into her face. She wore a red cloth coat stained beyond my imagination.

He was hollow-chested with long scraggly hair and a furtive air about him as though he expected to be arrested momentarily. His pants hung sadly where his buttocks should have been. Possibly he had pawned them to buy liquor. He had four or five long yellow teeth spaced like fence posts at strategic locations in his mouth. He had the odor of a long-abandoned barn.

To me they seemed quite compatible. Then, one evening she got in my taxi alone. She was only half-drunk but fully angry.

"Never marry a handsome man," she said to me. She ran through a list of unimaginative curses.

"Never marry a handsome man," she said again. I assured her that I would value her advice. She caught my sarcastic tone and advised me sullenly that I had better not take her the long way home.

"The young girls all go after him," she said, dripping on the leather upholstery. "He's back there with one of them now." She gestured over her shoulder where the neon sign of the bar glowed like a match in a row of matches. She sniffed mucously.

"My mother told me not to marry him because he was too good looking, but I did anyway, and I've been sorry ever since."

They lived in an old frame house that was molting like a chicken. Pieces were missing here and there and one window was bandaged with cardboard and electric tape. The front steps had mysteriously disappeared, or perhaps been kidnapped for a ransom that was never paid. From one hinge the storm door hung limply, like a broken wrist, about ten feet off the ground.

She counted her change carefully, then waddled around the corner of the house, like a bear. I have tried to imagine the back door of that house, but I can't.

Before she left she told me something I never suspected. It was a mixed marriage. He was a Cowichan, she a Songhees.

"Cowichans," she assured me gravely, "are all like that."

HOW I MISSED
THE MILLION DOLLAR
ROUND TABLE

Once, when I still believed in Chevrolet, apple pie, and the principle of pre-measured douche, I decided to sell life insurance. It looked like a quick way to make some money.

I chose to become employed by the Intercontinental Exchange Life Insurance and Income Protection Co., Inc. (Head Office: Wonderland, Mississippi). The company motto appeared in Latin on all their stationery. One of the veteran salesmen—he had a wooden leg and three bullet wounds in the abdomen—translated it as: "If God had insured his only son, it would have been with us." One of the bullet wounds was interdepartmental; the wooden leg was self-inflicted.

The branch manager, Lester Lively, gave off the amalgamated odors of Aqua Velva, Listerine, Old Spice deodorant, and pre-measured douche. He had freckles which had obviously been washed individually in a bowl of warm water and Ivory Snow, then scattered endearingly on his fresh, Norman Rockwell-boy-scout-baseball-playing face.

Before I was hired, I was courted, so to speak. Life insurance companies are like pimply freshmen with halitosis: they get very few dates. It is an age-old custom that prospective salesmen are wooed by branch managers, ac-

companied by their Ace Salesman, a jolly alcoholic, whose
freckles were years ago traded in for liver spots. Together
they dispense false promises, five-hour lunches, and excessive amounts of liquor. The prospective salesman
leaves the luncheon with lies and cliches clinging to his
suit like drunken spiders.

The Ace Salesman was named Michael Brink, or something equally television series-ish. He claimed to have
once played semi-pro baseball. After five drinks, he
equated selling life insurance with running the basepaths
of life. It sounded logical at the time.

The day after I started, Mr. Lively came to work looking very pale. The office grapevine reported that his
youngest son, an incorrigible little ankle-biter, had
poured milk on his father's freckles and eaten them while
watching the 7 AM rerun of *Leave It to Beaver*. Mr. Lively's
Norman Rockwell-boy-scout-baseball-playing face remained pallid for several days. He was nervous, received a
lot of phone calls, and often left the office without moving his magnetic button on the in-out board. Apparently,
they were watching junior's potty-do with tweezers
poised.

I sold life insurance policies to (a) my brother-in-law,
the one who tied tin cans to our wedding car, (b) a Portuguese house-painter who thought he was insuring his
half-ton truck, (c) the leader of the Coffin Chasers Motorcycle Gang, who had previously been named a terminally
undesirable risk by several companies, possibly because of
the real horse-shoes attached to the back of his denim
jacket. Rumor had it they were fastened to his back with
real nails. We reached an agreement. He promised not to
kill me; I transposed his first and second names on the ap-
plication, neglected to mention motorcycles, his knife

wound, or his eight brushes with gonorrhea. My company issued the policy. Three weeks later, Mr. Coffin Chaser was killed while playing "chicken" with a semi-trailer. Police had to use a vacuum cleaner to remove parts of him from the windscreen of a Fruehauf. It cost Intercontinental $25,000 for the policy and $25,000 double indemnity for accidental death.

From Wonderland, Mississippi, the white-suited company lawyers, on their magnolia-scented stationery, recommended that no claim be paid. Twelve Coffin Chasers, accompanied by their pet crowbars, made a business call on Mr. Lively. Their old ladies loitered in the waiting room; a couple of them practiced starting their chain saws.

Mr. Lively recommended that, in the interest of public relations, the company should pay the claim. They did. Wonderland, Mississippi recommended that they fire me. They did.

I was only $963,000 short of making the Million Dollar Round table.

Michael Brink died of a coronary at 43. His liver burst into flames when someone lit a bunsen burner during the autopsy. Lester Lively took to drinking Aqua Velva, Listerine, and pre-measured douche. Eventually, his liver joined the AFL-CIO. It first campaigned for better working conditions, then went on strike. Lester Lively went to a sanitarium. The last time I saw him he was selling encyclopedias door-to-door, and living in a house trailer up on blocks, in a trailer park with gravel streets and more children than Calcutta. His freckles had been long ago sold to pay his medical bills. I understand they were reconditioned and sold to an aspiring minister.

THE JOB

The building was in the warehouse district, brick long ago painted white, freckled now, paint curling like untended fingernails. The door said merely PERSONNEL. No company name. The ad in the newspaper read *Person with driver's license,* followed by the address.

Inside, the building was like a hangar, three stories high, with windows at the second and third levels suffering from occasional broken panes. In the ceiling were skylights muffled by years of cobwebs. The whole place smelled of oil and bird droppings. There were perhaps two dozen motorcycles of various makes and models scattered about. Toward the back of the building a fleet of vans was parked in a long row, their windshields like the sad eyes of children. The motorcycles and vans were all past their prime.

Part of the cement floor was turning back to gravel, the remainder was cracked and oil-stained. I heard the sound of a mechanic's dolly, and a man in soiled pin-striped overalls bumped from beneath a van, arms flailing as if he were swimming. A pigeon fluttered in the rafters.

When I stood up, I saw he was fortyish, with a ragged crewcut, a cigarette dangling from his pouty lower lip.

"I came about the job," I said, in reply to his questioning glance.

"Oh yeah," he said. "Lemme see your driver's license."

I showed it to him. He turned it over a couple of times

with oily fingers, compared the photo to my face, then said, "You'll do. Wanna start tonight?"

"What is it I do?"

"You ride a bike," he said, pointing at the congregation of motorcycles.

"To where?"

He looked at me as though I were stupid. Perhaps he had recently explained the intricacies of the job to someone who looked like me. Exasperated, he walked to one of the bikes, an elderly Harley, leapt on and started it up. It didn't appear to have a muffler and was out of tune.

"I'll assign a four-square-block area," he yelled over the rumble of the bike. "From nine in the evening to three in the morning you just ride around those streets on your bike. Stick to your assigned area and everything will be fine. There's a pump out back to gas up. You sign in and out over there," pointing to a greasy, black, ledger-like book lying among tools on a workbench.

"But why?" I asked. "What's my job?"

He shut off the Harley. "You live in a residential district?" he asked.

"Yeah."

"Well, isn't there a motorcycle without a muffler that travels around your neighborhood?"

I stopped to think for a minute before I replied. "Yeah, there is," I finally said.

"Well, you don't think those things happen by accident, do you?"

"You mean you supply motorcycles to drive around and keep people awake, make them mad, disturb their TV reception?"

"You got it. In the winter we use vans. The drivers sit

them at the curb, work their wheels into the ice until
they're stuck, then spin their wheels and roar their engines for an hour or so."

"Always outside my house," I said.

"Right. Probably they're three or four doors away, but if we do a good job, everybody thinks it's in front of their house."

"I've never driven a bike before," I said.

"I could give you an ambulance," he went on. "We have a couple, but you have to cover a twelve-block-square area. The consolation is you get to turn the siren (he pronounced it 'si-reen') up to full wail."

"Are you a government agency?"

"We're not sure. It's all very hush-hush. My paycheck comes from a holding company; it would take twenty years to find out who owns it. Personally, I think we're sponsored by the Southern Bapist Convention — there are thirteen million of those suckers, did you know that? — or maybe Oral Roberts. Duke — he's the night man — thinks we're CIA or FBI, but I don't think so. You'd have to be religious to want to make *everybody* miserable.

"Just driving, that's all?"

"Well, you burn a lot of rubber, make quick stops and starts. Just try to remember how the driver in your area does it. Now, you want it or not? I got a muffler to tear off and a couple of motors to get out of tune before the nightshift."

"I think I'll pass. Thanks anyway."

"Suit yourself. You can't change your mind though. If you come back tomorrow, you'll find a sash-and-door plant here."

48   I've often wondered if that was true. Everytime a motorcycle roars past my bedroom window, or a stuck van
screams at the curb, I make a mental note to go back and
check. But in the morning it all seems like a dream.

Part Three
The Redemption Center

THE REDEMPTION CENTER

The shop opened on a Monday morning. Over the weekend the defunct Chinese Cafe had been gutted. Sheets of white newsprint had been taped over the windows until all that could be seen from the street was an occasional shadow behind the snowy façade. The shop was located in a block on E. Hastings Street, close to the heart of skid row, where the ever-present wind blows doorways full of dead leaves and dry newspapers. As I watched from across the street, a sign, hand lettered in blue watercolor, was inserted between the newsprint and the window. It read:

ALL SUFFERING IS REDEMPTIVE
Luke 23:4

I have lived enough of my life in cheap hotels, with a Gideon Bible as a bedfellow, to know the quote was more fancy than fact. I walked across the street and, kicking debris aside, pulled open the much-dented aluminum door. I would be their first customer.

The gloomy interior was coldly empty except for a small counter to my immediate left, the kind one might find in a failing convenience store, cheap wood and glass, scratched and abused. Behind the counter were two people, a young man who looked like a pharmacist: white smock, sculptured golden hair, clear complexion. The woman beside him was cheerleader fresh, also dressed in white, with a pretty, pink carnation of a mouth. The cavernous room smelled of grease, lumber, and vacancy.

"Welcome, Brother," the young man said.

"What are you selling?" I asked.

"Selling?" he said, looking at me questioningly. "We do more buying than selling. What have you brought us?"

"Nothing," I said.

"Nothing?" he replied.

A dishevelled Indian with sores on his face pushed through the door and approached the counter. He clutched a filthy paper bag in his hand.

"Yes?" said the girl, smiling.

The Indian thrust the bag at her and slurred a couple of words I did not understand.

"Why yes, I think that can be arranged," the girl said, and reaching under the counter brought out a drum, handmade, beaded, expensive. The Indian smiled, and embraced it to his body with one large, shaking hand.

"Thank you," he said clearly, turned and strode away.

"If you didn't bring anything for us," the young man said, "you'll have to step aside. We expect to be very busy today."

Already a half-dozen people were lined up, nearly to the door: a shopping-bag lady, a couple of elderly winos, a one-legged man I had often seen begging change at the corner of Hastings and Main, a hooker-junkie with pinprick eyes, a sad-faced young woman with shrill yellow hair who I had observed working as a pickpocket.

One of the winos handed over a corked beer bottle, full of a murky liquid; he received a book, a hardcover with a glossy dust jacket. The hooker swayed unsteadily for a

few seconds, her eyes fighting to close; she dug deep in
her purse, handed the girl a fat manila envelope. The girl
passed something back to her with a surreptitious movement and a knowing smile.

"How do they find you?" I whispered to the young
man.

"How long would it take them to discover a new pawn
shop or a new liquor store?" he replied, nodding to the
girl to indicate he would be busy for a few moments.
"They have to move quickly, they know we'll only be
here for one day."

"But how do they know?"

"How do geese know when to migrate? Why do the
trees explode?" he replied, a half-smile on his handsome
face.

"What do they bring you?" I asked.

"You mean you don't know?"

"Have no idea."

"Then how did *you* find us?"

"I watched them emptying the cafe over the weekend,
watched you put up the sign."

"No one who doesn't understand our purpose is supposed to see. You're sure you have nothing for me?"

"Like what?"

He paused a long time. "Your seeing us must be a fluke
of nature, like dragging in a radio station from a city two
thousand miles away."

"Like what?" I repeated.

"Like pain."

"Pain?"

"The sign," he said, pointing. "All suffering *is* redemptive. They bring in their pain, their fear, their guilt, their

frustration, their panic . . ."

"And trade it for what?"

"Whatever they desire most. Whatever will ease their pain."

"But who are these that they are so special?"

"There are those," and he waved his hand to indicate the forlorn creatures in the lineup, "who take on the pain of strangers."

"Intentionally?"

"They don't realize why they do what they do."

"But you do?"

"Indeed."

"What about the rest of us? All those that don't see? Don't we have enough pain to know you?"

"Not so much that you can't cope. That's because these people gather up your pain when you strew it behind you, breathe the odor of it in your wake; they purge the bodies of strangers, like draining boils, until they themselves are filled to bursting. When they can stand no more, they bring what they've collected to us, pass away the poison, and for a few moments are pain free."

"What do you give them in return? What do *you* pass to *them* from this magic store?"

"For a few moments their most secret wish blooms in front of them like a rose studded with dew. We give them whatever they ask for. It is never unreasonable."

"But what?"

"It may only be a memory, a picture of a loved one as they were long ago, or they may request someting more tangible. Sometimes we are surprised, but we never let on. When you have nothing it takes very little to satisfy."

All the long afternoon and into the cold evening a gray

and motley line of derelicts trembled outside the Redemption Center: hoodlums and hookers, addicts pale as ca-
mellias, old men hunched like turtles inside their over-
coats — the forgotten, the forsaken, the carriers of pain.

They inched forward, transporting their suffering in
jars, bags, bread wrappers. Some clutched furtively at inside pockets, some consigned the pain to colored bottles,
or bore it in a can with a hand clamped over the top, as a
boy might imprison a frog.

I stood in a doorway across the street, shivering myself,
knowing the Redemption Center would close at mid-
night, that in the morning it would be nothing but another vacant building on the chill street. Still, I stayed to
the very end, trying to guess which frail soul might be
siphoning off the pain of my existence, allowing me to
go on.

MARCO IN PARADISE

Marco Ferlinghetti spends his life getting picked out of police lineups. The police collar Marco nearly every day. He is not hard to find for he is never more than two blocks from the corner of Hastings and Main in Vancouver at any time in his life. Marco stands sullen in the middle of the lineup, eyelids drooping, while behind two-way glass victims and witnesses scrutinize. On one especially productive day Marco was positively identified as a flasher, a hit-and-run driver, a burglar, and a peeping tom.

The rationale of the police is that if a potential witness can pass over Marco for someone else, then the identification is likely to stick. The reason that Marco is such a popular choice is that he looks exactly the way people think a criminal should look. He has scraggly, receding hair, protruding eyes, no chin to speak of, and is always in need of a shave. His teeth are yellow, his nose hooked; he wears a dirty trenchcoat, baggy pants and sneakers. Marco Ferlinghetti is the middle-class idea of a child molester, pimp, pusher, and petty thief.

Marco did indeed do time a few years ago for the innocuous crime of selling a marijuana cigarette to an undercover cop. While he was in prison (Marco was treated rather harshly, partly because of his looks and partly because the undercover cop was standing outside an elementary school when he made the buy), he decided to learn a trade. Behind the walls he learned to be a cannon (a professional pickpocket) and practices his trade with a solemn efficiency. His stall (an assistant who distracts the intended victim, usually by bumping into them) is his girlfriend, whom he calls Jackson, a bedraggled little hype in jeans, boots, and a halter that exposes most of her breasts. Jackson always looks as if she is about to ask someone for directions.

The police know of Marco's profession but live and let live as long as he keeps himself available for daily lineups.

A few weeks ago, Marco, in all his grimy splendor, crabwalked into a Toronto-Dominion Bank on Granville Street, several blocks from Hastings and Main, and presented the teller with a note which was clearly printed but poorly spelled and punctuated. Marco, the proud holder of a B.Com. from the University of British Columbia, walked away with several thousand dollars.

The police pulled in an assortment of known bank robbers; they also pulled in Marco Ferlinghetti.

"That's him!" said the robbed teller.

"That's him!" said the assistant bank manager.

"That's him!" said an elderly lady who had been in line behind Marco.

The police politely thanked them for their trouble.

A few days later Marco limped into the Main Street Police Station and approached the sergeant in charge of police lineups.

"I'd like to take a little time off," he said deferentially. "I think I picked a rotten pocket, if you know what I mean. Came into a large amount of bread, but the empty pocket belonged to the Mob. There are nasty rumors on the street."

"You go ahead, Marco," said the police officer. The sergeant had a soft spot in his heart for petty criminals like Marco. He didn't like the Mob either. "Just be sure you settle around here when you come back. You're very valuable to us."

Marco and Jackson caught the next flight for Honolulu. But even in paradise, dressed in a Hawaiian shirt, with a lei of waxen orchids around his neck, Marco Ferlinghetti looked like a criminal. His third day on Waikiki, Marco was picked up and displayed in a police lineup. Late at night, wallets, picked clean as fish skeletons, glow whitely in the alleys of Honolulu.

VOYEUR

With shallow breath I wait for night. This place is full of my cast off parts. I dare not touch them, they are the past and cannot be modified. My mouth is stuffed with pink petals, too sweetly full to speak. Frost glitters on me. I am coated in crystal, delicate as new ice. My movements stealthy, cold, so cold. I am a voyeur, peering in on life. I absorb what no one will miss, breathe bits of the eternal into my greedy face. I am addicted to other people's lives.

Once, I used to be someone. I went to work, I worked at night. The streets were always blue and cold when I walked home at dawn to my furnished room. My identity shrunk until it was only a seed, rattling side to side in my gourd body.

I destroyed my birth certificate, driver's license, credit cards, and photos of people. In a motel room, I dipped my fingertips in acid.

Afterward I walked through a building, trying doors until I found one unlocked. I toured the apartment, touching nothing, just observing how other people existed, drawing their leftover life into my body, feeling a rising sexual excitement at the dark portrait of clothes strewn on a bedroom floor.

Those who see me sense I will shatter if they speak. I shimmer in silence. The last one who spoke to me was a motorist. I was in his way. He didn't care if he broke me. His lips, behind glass, like medical books locked in a case, formed pebble words which missed me as I ran.

A plastic cheater, slim and sensuous, is my constant companion. If I am caught, if I am a criminal, all the media will be able to say of me is . . . his only possession was a plastic cheater . . . a solid, formal statement, like a "reliable diplomatic source" would report a political coup.

Sometimes I am seen where I should not be, as a shape entering a locked room or a shadow on a blind. Then sirens come like neon birds through the night, while I in my terror merge with stone and plaster.

While people sleep, I and my plastic lover waft our way into rooms where I suck up life through a crystal straw. As I walk my footprints rise from the carpet. I collect odors and my eyes remember. There is never a trace that I have ever been. I touch nothing, knowing that one object moved could change the course of history. The yellow race might rule the world because I moved a sprawling, silent shirt from the back of a chair.

I enter a barber shop where the pole, like me, hides behind a glass façade. I breathe in tonic, soap, lather, and the clipper-oil smell, gobble up bits of life that hum in the air. I will all around me to live, the pole to twist and turn, the dryers to dry, the lather dispenser to dispense, the clippers to clip . . . but, I have no identity, I am no one. The lather is marble and the clippers are turned fool-golden by the street lights. I pull in every detail with my poultice eyes. I appropriate the reflection of a girl's button as she walks by the shop, only a sheet of glass and a layer of crystal separating us.

There was a girl once, cool and ominous, tense as a rain cloud. We never spoke. We touched our bodies, glass to glass, a passionless tinkling on cold sheets. When she was

gone, I sat for days absorbing what she had been: Drawing in her perfume, cherishing the spot where her head
dented the pillow, studying a small golden hair, curled
like a snail on the sheet. The violets of her eyes had grown
into the pillow. I touched nothing, knowing that I
would disappear forever if I so much as rearranged the
cigarette ends in the ashtray.

Sometimes I stand and watch people sleep, so close I
can see their eyes darting behind closed lids. I feel their
breath fog my hands, and smell the sweet odors of identity. So clever, so clever, I drift, a shadow without a
body, as moonlight reflects my many facets, and, far off, a
cat screams in an alley.

KING OF
THE STREET

A little buzzsaw of a wind chews at my ankles, whips dirt
and sand up at my face, chases papers along the concrete
until they flutter into store fronts like wounded birds.
Though I'm over half a block behind him, I recognize
King's strut as he hoofs along Hastings Street toward the
Sunshine Hotel. He hesitates for just an instant at the
door of the Sunshine's bar. I can see his lips curse as he
glances around quickly to see if anyone has noticed. Two
big whores wearing halters, shorts, and knee boots,
patrol the sidewalk. Neither looks at King. But I know,
and King knows, that only cons and ladies wait for someone to open doors for them.

"Hey, King," I shout. "Wait up!" But he disappears
into the Sunshine, probably heading to the back of the bar
to find Hacksaw.

I lope after him. I'll catch up while his eyes are getting
used to the cavelike darkness, while his other senses ingest
the warm-sour odor of beer, the smell of smoky upholstery.

King has been in the slam for almost a year. I'm betting
this is his first day out.

2

It was Hacksaw I got to know first. Contrary to popular opinion, even bikers get lonely.

The Sunshine Bar is right in the heart of the drag, and is to the skid row area what the stock exchange is to the financial district. If you can't arrange to get it at the Sunshine, it can't be got. And, if you can smoke it, snort it, shoot it, fuck it, wear it, or drive it, Hacksaw, the head honcho of the Coffin Chasers can get it for you.

Empty, the Sunshine is big enough to drive buffalo through, but it's never empty. The atmosphere of the Sunshine is like the inside of a bee hive. The walls have faded murals of girls in grass skirts dancing against a background of blue sky and palm trees. The dancing girls have twenty years accumulated fly specks on them, just like a lot of the clientele. The front half of the bar is for anybody, but the back door and all the tables around it are reserved for the Coffin Chasers.

I've been dropping in to the Sunshine a couple of times a week for years. I usually sit close to the biker's section — it's called the Coffin Corner — but never in it unless I'm invited. If some stranger wanders in and goes to sit at one of their tables, one of the CC's ambles over and speaks without moving his lips. "If you want to live long and die happy, get the fuck out of this section," he says. Ordinary citizens, unless they have a death wish, tend not to argue with bikers.

I'm a voyeur when it comes to the bikers. I sit near their tables, eavesdrop as much as I can. I'm jealous of the women they attract. I'd give anything to behave as fearlessly as they do. But I never will. "There are only two kinds of men," Hacksaw said to me one night, "those who are bikers, and those who wish they were."

I agree.

"Come here," Hacksaw said to me one night. He was

alone in the CC's section, slumped down, sitting on his neck, looking like a denim bean-bag chair with a head. Hacksaw has been described as "300 lbs. of hate, with the disposition of a rhino."

After he beckoned to me, I picked up my beer and climbed the two carpeted steps to the Coffin Corner. Hacksaw motioned me to a chair; an honor in itself.

"I hear you write," he said. I was surprised that Hacksaw even knew I existed, let alone that he knew anything about me.

I nodded, swallowing.

"I could tell you some stories," he said. His voice emanated from somewhere near his four-inch-square brass belt buckle. He wore oil-splattered jeans, black biker's boots; what must have been a size 60 black tee-shirt covered his bulk. Gold lettering on the shirt read Harley Fucking Davidson.

"I'm probably not that kind of writer," I said, "but I'd be happy to listen any time you want to talk." It is a universal truth that *everybody*, absolutely *everybody*, thinks they have stories to tell.

"I don't understand what you're doin' here though," Hacksaw went on, waving his hand to show he meant not just the bar, but the area of the city, the street.

I shrugged my shoulders. Remained silent.

"Are you them or us?" When I looked puzzled he went on. "Are you straight or street?"

"I've been both," I said. "I didn't know I had to choose."

"You can't be both. Down there," and he pointed to the front of the bar, "You're swimmin' at the bottom of the barrel. This place is full of stumble-fucks, junkie-

whores, winos . . . You stand out like a fuckin' wrist-
watch hippie . . ."

"Winos and whores are some of my favorite people . . .
not necessarily in that order . . ." I said while Hacksaw
stared coldly at me.

We talked for about an hour, until the Coffin Corner
filled up with bikers and their ladies. The lot outside the
back door looked like a chrome junkyard; the flashy
motorcycles rumbled like guarddogs. Hacksaw, without
ever coming right out and stating it, let me know that he
was literate to some degree. Something he obviously
didn't want his cronies to know, for he stayed on safe sub-
jects—dope, sex and motorcycles, when any of them
were within hearing. I remember thinking that if I had
nerve enough to riff through the saddle bags on his chop-
per I might find a hardcover book or two stashed among
his wrenches.

"You're droolin'," Hacksaw said to me at one point,
grinning. I was staring too long at a lithe, dark-haired
girl with amber eyes, who had tattoos from her wrists to
the ragged edge of her cutoff demin vest.

"It shows?"

"I can fix you up no problem."

"Not tonight, thanks," I said with tremendous effort.
There are iron strings attached to every favor a guy like
Hacksaw performs. I wasn't ready to be in his debt.

3

In that way out-going strangers in a bar have of drawing people at nearby tables into their conversations, King
reeled me in, like scooping a fish from a puddle. I'd seen
him around the Sunshine for a month or two. He made it

plain he was from the East and considered himself a cut above the locals, but he did it in such an ingratiating way that he offended no one. He'd scored himself two chicks, neither one very pretty, but diligent whores who stayed on the street until they turned as many tricks as King thought they should.

Some guys attract whores. King did. I wish I did. If a whore approaches me in a bar or on the street it is to ask if I want to go out: street talk for "Do you want to fuck and pay for it?"

When I stop to think about it I realize that I have never chosen a friend. I am always chosen. Male or female. My ex-wife chose me. Every lover I've ever had chose me. King chose me. Though you couldn't get him to admit it through torture, he likes me because I'm literate, introspective, shy, all the things King is not. We are friends though. He operates at the most primitive levels. But then everything on the street is at a primitive level.

The fall King took came after he scored a third chick, a sweet thing named Lannie; smoke-blond hair, a sensual mouth, no illusions about what she is or does. Her problem was too big a fondness for junk. King would have straightened her out. But Ginny, the number one chick, got jealous and set him up.

4

"Even sociopaths need friends," Lannie said to King one evening. I noticed that she and I were the only one who could tease King and get away with it.

"Hey, if you subtracted my I.Q. from the National Debt, the budget would be balanced," said King.

"He believes that," said Lanny.

"What can I say?" said King, smiling like he was accepting an award.

"King's never read anything longer than a street sign,"
said Lannie.

King is tall, raw-boned, moves like a sleek animal. He
has dark, curly hair that floods over his collar and fore-
head. He *is* super-intelligent; he has total recall of conversations held months or years before. His eyes are a bitter
blue, as if they're filled with metal filings. He always appears to be adding up unseen columns of figures, making
calculations.

At his trial King's defense was "If she didn't give her
money to me she'd have given it to somebody else," a
premise that is completely valid on the street, but is not
covered in any judges' manual. King drew 18 months for
what was called Living off the Avails of Prostitution.

Surprisingly, King was not bitter. "If you can't do the
time, don't do the crime," he philosophized. But his eyes
glinted like railroad tracks under moonlight as he was saying it.

I could have appeared at the trial as a witness for King.
I was there the night he hooked up with Ginny. She came
to him. I was at the next table when she sat down beside
King, flashed a C-note she'd acquired by selling her ser-
vices, and offered it to King, snuggling against his arm.
"If you were my old man, there'd be a couple of these
every day," she said, simpering, leaking smoke through
her teeth.

I was practically exploding with lust at the thought.
But King was cool as November. He let her sweat it out;
he fingered the C-note, unfolded it, played with it,
tucked it under a beer glass on the table instead of putting
it in his pocket.

"How do you do it?" I asked him once.

"Never rush into anything with a broad, man. Let 'em know you don't fucking care a lick about them," he said. "Those kind of chicks know deep down they're not worth shit. It turns them on to have to crawl for a little attention. Listen, you fucking guys who read big books and don't know what's going down on the street got it all wrong about the relationship between whores and their old men. These chicks don't do anything they don't want to do; they never give away money they don't want to part with. Hell, most of them can't wait to give away their trick money. A good old man just keep his ladies happy, and keeps them from mainlining too much junk into their arms.

"You got to understand the psychology involved, and it ain't in your fucking books, man. I never roughed up a chick who didn't crave to be roughed up. Back East I had this chickie used to come to me with her belt in her hand, pull down her jeans and hand me the strap. Man, did we get it on when I was finished with her."

5

About a month after King began serving his time, Ginny kept a date first with a hot cap (heroin about a hundred times stronger than the watered down shit that's usually on the street) then with the coroner.

"A tragic loss, " drawled Hacksaw from under half-closed lids. "In the downward order of the universe there are cockroaches, slugs, shit, snitches, and bare pavement," and he smiled like a lion that had just eaten its fill of something less fortunate.

I was the one who introduced King to Hacksaw. King

mentioned that he needed some wheels and had the bread
to buy them.

"You're not gonna pay full price?" I said.

"Hey, what's money for?" said King, patting his vest pocket.

"I'll introduce you to Hacksaw," I volunteered.

"I don't know. I usually leave sleeping bikers lie." But he didn't stop me.

"You just put out the word on what you want and in a day or two it'll appear in the back parking lot. Two-thirds off retail. Hacksaw doesn't scoff it himself; he doesn't even hold; he just takes his cut."

I visited King in the slammer, twice. I went to tell him about Ginny, but of course he already knew.

"What can I say?" said King, grinning. "As you sow, so shall you reap.

"Like they say, man, the sun don't shine on the same dog's ass every day. By the way, I've joined the Bible Thumpers." He lowered his voice. "Hell of a P.R. move. Good for a couple of months off this gig."

The second time I offered to take Lannie.

"Nah," she said, "visitin' the joint always makes me sad."

When I told Hacksaw I was taking the bus out to the prison he said, "How much money do you make from writing stories?"

"I haven't made any yet," I admitted.

"For chrissakes," said Hacksaw, reaching deep into his boot and producing a plastic folder full of credit cards and I.D. "Rent yourself a car. Buy yourself some threads; you look like a bum. Go to the bank, go to seven or eight banks and get some cash. Then flush this stuff down a sewer."

What the hell! Being indebted to Hacksaw probably wasn't as bad as it seemed.

6

"Hey, King, you leave your fucking hearing behind the walls?" I say as I catch up with him in the middle of the bar. A pathetic little half-breed girl is trying to dance on a tiny stage covered in green indoor-outdoor. She has a home-made tattoo on her butt reads: Property of Big Frank. Her sad little titties point at the floor.

King shakes hands, clasping my arm with his free hand. I think he is genuinely happy to see me. He is thinner, his clothes hang at odd angles.

"Come on," he says, "I'm goin' to see the Hacksaw. I need some new threads." He stares around the smoky bee-hive. "Place is still jammed with college graduates, I see."

We wait at the bottom of the steps until we catch Hacksaw's eye. It doesn't matter who you are, if you don't wear the club colors you don't go up the steps unless you're invited. Hacksaw's newest lady is squashed up next to him, a snubnosed chick with freckles and wheat-colored hair, must be at least sixteen. Up top she's wearing only a denim vest with the CC's colors on the back; she's busy licking Hacksaw's ear. He has his left hand all the way down the front of her jeans.

Hacksaw buys a round and we visit for a while. King lets his needs be known. "Who's boosting these days?" he asks.

"The Fox," says Hacksaw. "See the guy with the red hair and beard," and he points to the middle of the lower section where this laid-back lookin' dude has his chair

tipped back and his Dingos parked on a table. "Works
with a Black chick. They're cool. How long you been
away?"

"Almost a year."

"I figured. When you want wheels you know who to
see." King nods. "Make it within a week and I'll throw
this in for a couple of days," and he uses his right hand to
lift the kid's vest and show her little, freckled tits. "Nice,
eh?"

"Nice, Hacksaw. You shouldn't do that to a guy who's
only a few hours out of the slam."

"Take her back to the john for a few minutes. She sucks
like silk."

"Maybe later," says King. We head down the steps
toward the Fox's table.

Same old Hacksaw, wants to have everybody in his
debt.

"Hacksaw sent me," says King, pulling up a chair
backwards, straddling it.

"I seen you jawing with him," says the Fox. He is
rightly named: only about 5'7", skinny, with a shag of
red hair and a scraggily beard. His eyes are golden, and
move around fast like a chicken's. King explains what he
wants.

"I'll alert my boost," says the Fox, "back in two," and
he signals the waiter to drop us a beer each.

Five minutes later the Fox is back. "Let's go
shopping," he says, clapping his hands together. King
picked a department store on Granville Street, in the high
rent district. We cruise the men's wear department and
he picks out a complete wardrobe, topped by this nifty
$550 suede suit. The Fox makes mental notes of types and

sizes, tapping his head just in front of his left ear to show he has the information stored there. He takes the suede suit off the rack, holds it up to inspect it, puts it back with the hanger facing opposite to its neighbors.

"Where's your cannon?" I ask.

"She's around," says the Fox.

I look up to the mezzanine to where a coffee shop over-looks the business floor. A slim Black girl with tight, corn-rowed hair and a long skirt sits staring down at us.

"Strong?" asks King.

"Can slap a table-model typewriter between her thighs and boogie out of the store like she was being chased."

"Class," says King. The Fox nods in agreement.

"Meet me back at the Sunshine at seven," he says to King. "We'll have everything for you by then," and he smiles though his thin, red mustache covers his upper lip completely.

7

Outside the store, King and I part company. I am half way back to my room when my teeth start to itch and I develop a feeling as if someone is staring hard at the back of my neck. Some guys claim they can tell when they enter a room is someone is carrying a piece. Other guys claim they can smell cops. To me there is something about the Fox that smells bad. Maybe it takes an outsider to spot an outsider. I circle around and head back to the store. Everything seems okay. The suede suit is exactly as we left it. I move to the mezzanine coffee shop and take a table with a view.

Two nervous hours later my hunch is rewarded. I watch as a sad-looking man in a brown-striped suit emerges from the dressing room area, takes the suede suit off the rack and carries it into the back. He has store-dick written all over him.

As I head back toward the Sunshine I wonder how I should handle the situation. The Fox and his lady are almost certainly undercover heat. They won't hit King or Hacksaw today. Sometimes these types make hundreds of deals before the ax falls. An operation can go on for a year or more, then in the dark of night the heat covers the drag like a sponge and slurps up every small timer who ever custom ordered a five-finger-bargain or dealt an ounce of grass. But the Black chick, Cora, is supposed to be a junkie. That puts a whole new face on the operation. A lot of street people, Hacksaw included, could take a big fall. I'm clean, so I could warn the Fox that I'm onto him. If I did, he and his chick would disappear off the street fast as the steam that huffs up out of manholes. But they're not smart enough to leave well enough alone; they'd still drag the streets, use the evidence they've collected.

I guess I'm gonna have to decide if I'm *them* or *us*. "There's one law on the streets and one law in the suburbs. If the heat would only realize that it would be a lot better world." I realize that I'm quoting King. Well, maybe he's right.

At the Sunshine I head directly for the Coffin Corner. I don't wait to be invited up the steps. As I drop into a chair across from Hacksaw the corner gets very quiet.

"Get rid of the jailbait," I say, "we've got to talk."

A couple of Coffin Chasers are reaching for the shanks in their boots, but Hacksaw stops them with a movement of his head. He unwinds the blond and pushes her away. "Bring Hacksaw fifty dollars," he says to the chickie. She pouts. He grabs a handful of ass and holds on. She yells as he gives her a push toward the back door. "And make it quick." She scuttles off like a dog that's just been kicked.

Hacksaw sniffs the fingers he's had down the front of Blondie's jeans, and smiles. "It better be important, my friend," he says to me.

"Could be," he says, after he's heard what I have to say. "The Man gets trickier every year. "Be cool, I know how to handle this. Like that old joke, try to pretend nothing unusual is happening. All you got to do is what I tell you . . ."

8

I disappear until about an hour before the deal is due to go down. King is with Lannie at her favorite table near the door. She is stoned, nodding into her beer, her neck whiplashing every thirty seconds or so. A john comes over, taps her awake; she gets up, walking like she has rubber ankles, takes his arm and they head for the door. She's wearing jeans and her sweater has stains on it.

"She's startin' to look like a whore," says King. "Guess I hit the bricks just in time. "Lannie's a class chick," he goes on, "all she needs is an aggressive old man to keep her in line. What I like about Lannie is she can handle a john or a deal even when she's blissed to the gills. Her head clears when there's bread on the line."

When she come back to the table, King puts an arm around her shoulder, pulls her and her chair close up to him. "Later tonight," he says, "I'm gonna get me a room, some good smoke, a bottle of Three Crown and a lady who like to fuck up a storm. You know of a chick who might like to join me?"

Lannie blows smoke and licks her lips. "Why don't you cross the room off your list, we can use mine," and she rubs her nose against his shoulder.

"Suits me," says King, "but first some business. You know the Fox's woman?"

"Sure, Cora . . ."

"She a junkie?"

"Yeah. She buys . . ."

"You ever seen her fix?"

"She's on the stuff, man . . ."

'You ever seen the needle in her arm?"

"No."

He clues Lanny into the scene. She looks at me in a new light, actually seeing me; she smiles an off-center smile.

"Here's what I want you to do," says King. "Cora's on her way here. Go outside and get a couple of girls you can trust. The CC's want to talk to Cora but they don't want to be seen snatching her off the street. And make sure you keep her hands in sight, she might be carrying a piece."

Lannie is out the door a minute later.

"Blissed or not, she's a good lady," says King.

Seven o'clock comes and goes. I have purposely sat with my back to Fox's table, but every few minutes I sneak a glance at him. His feet are on the floor now, and he is nervous, doing a little dance. I bet he'd like to be up and pacing, but he's got to pretend to be cool.

Lannie comes in the front door, catches King's eye, winks, and goes out again.

He draws his index finger across his throat in a quick, slashing motion. "Fucking snitch," he says, without moving his lips.

Following Hacksaw's instructions, I go and make a phone call on the single pay phone by the front door. I then accompany King over to Fox's table.

"Where's your cannon?" King says, standing close beside the Fox, giving him a pretend frisk, enough to establish he doesn't have a piece under his shirt. About his only chance right now is to haul out a piece, fire a shot into the ceiling, and wait for the management to call in the street cops.

"She's a little late, man. You know you can't trust junkies," and he gives us a little shark of a smile, though his eyes are blinking ten times a second. "What's with the frisk. You heat or something?"

"Or something," says King. "Fox, you and your lady have made a lot of people unhappy."

"I don't follow," says Fox. "Don't worry. Cora will be along with your stuff."

"No she won't." The Fox's skin is pale even under his beard and there are stains under the arms of his dark blue shirt. "They must have told you what happens to snitches, undercover, fucking pigs. You must know how a chick gets a few straightforward words carved into her body before she o.d.'s. You must have heard about how they find snitches with their cock and balls stuffed in their mouths. That's done while they're still alive, Fox. As a warning to the Man not to put any more snitches on the street. But they always do. Guys like you figure they're smarter than guys like us," and he stares at Fox, expressionless. I realize I'm looking at Fox the same way, not a trace of emotion on my face.

Fox is staring around is desperation. Hacksaw and

most of the CC's are between him and the back door. A
couple of Coffin Chasers, like leather-covered sides if
beef, hang on each side of the front entrance.

"If you're a snitch, man, you got one chance, and that's
to get to the pay phone and call your friends to come and
get you." King picks a dime off the green terry-cloth
table top and holds it out to Fox. He snatches it and darts
toward the phone.

"Thanks," he mumbles.

"Luck," says King, then gives me a look. I nod.

He'll need it. I jammed the phone with a slug before we
visited Fox's table.

Part Four

There is Some That is Crazier Than Winos

THE RESURRECTION OF TROUTFISHING IN AMERICA SHORTY

I was wandering in the International District in Seattle, heading vaguely in the direction of the ballpark where a team called the Mariners play in a musty, dusky basement of a stadium. I stepped into an alley to toss my Pepsi Light can into a heap of cloth and paper. A rat scuttled, like a house shivering in the dark.

Trout Fishing in America Shorty sat grimy and stubble-faced in a ratty old wheelchair, a cheap wheelchair with the chrome worn off; it was a fast-food-restaurant-of-a-wheelchair, cheap and easy and tasteless, full of empty calories and Trout Fishing in America Shorty.

Trout Fishing in America Shorty was wearing a pair of floppy khaki-colored work pants which were badly in need of a steelworker to fill them out. The stained, filthy pant legs trickled across the seat of the wheelchair and groped toward the ground, thin and empty, bitter at never having known the feel of a foot or a leg.

Trout Fishing in America Shorty clutched a brown-bagged bottle, tightly as if it were a faithful pet, and stared at me from his rotting face which was the color of ripe strawberries.

"You're a famous literary character," I said.

Trout Fishing in American Shorty tipped up the

brown-bagged bottle. His dirty hand was small and blunt as a child's, the same color as the brown paper.

"Don't you know that you are a hero of literature?" I went on. "A General MacArthur of storytelling. A Black Beauty, a Rin Tin Tin, a Nick Adams, a Garp."

"Fuck off," said Trout Fishing in America Shorty, his eyes tiny as ants in his alcohol-poisoned face.

"No wonder Richard Brautigan wanted to put you in a packing crate and ship you to Chicago to live with Nelson Algren. You're not very polite, you know?"

"There is some that is crazier than winos," said Trout Fishing in America Shorty, and with the hand that was not holding the bottle he turned his fast-food-restaurant-of-a-cheelchair to the side so he would not have to look at me.

And why not? Sitting in a moist alley in Seattle in the summer with a brown-bagged bottle for company is not all bad. Richard Brautigan is in Montana. Nelson Algren is dead. So dead that Trout Fishing in America Shorty might go unclaimed for months at the Chicago Railroad Terminal if someone shipped him there.

"There is some that is crazier than winos," a profound thought. Perhaps it could replace "In God We Trust" on our currency. A phrase like that would tend to keep America humble. And if Lincoln were alive I'm sure he could work it into the Gettysburg Address.

THE LETTER WRITER

I write letters at strange and inopportune times: at baseball games, in the back of taxis, while lining up a putt on the sixteenth green, and as I am now, while supposedly sleeping in that blue-steel span of morning just before sunrise. I am addicted to chocolate cookies, hot baths, and girls in bluejeans. Whichever I have had last I want least. Whichever I have been longest without I want most. In between I write letters. I am going to write a letter to Christie who is not far away. In fact, she is sleeping beside me. A peach-petal kind of sleep, her breath soft as a bird. She half-smiles, dreaming perhaps of the time, as a child, when a bus driver bought her an ice cream cone. She says it made her very happy because she had not expected to have any ice cream that day.

I lie on my stomach, my pen and paper on the floor, while the room turns from black to stove-lid blue, the color of trolley wires. Christie's clothes are near my writing hand: her jeans, her white blouse with the little-girl sleeves, her panties which have Tuesday embroidered on the crotch, although it won't be Tuesday for several days. The clothes emit warmth. Christie's clothes are like that—warm and full of love even when they are hanging in her closet or lying on the floor near my empty page.

Although I am a compulsive letter writer, I find that it is not much fun writing to people I know. Friends fail to understand that the truly dedicated letter writer does not write about everyday things, but about the perceptions which those mundane happenings and situations create and scatter over him like stardust. Friends read what I write to them, think *what a weird letter,* and out of duty write back. Their parents have taught them that it is bad manners not to answer a letter, no matter how strange. In reply they say something like: the kids all have colds, John got his raise, I am taking a night-school course on how to build boats in bottles, I think I am pregnant again.

I correspond almost exclusively with women. Most men frighten me. They tend to slap people on the back, they don't spell very well, and there are often shadows of crescent wrenches and ball bearings on their stationery.

I write mostly to strangers. To find them, I go through the City Directory and pick out a lonely name. Sometimes I pretend I am a disc jockey with a soothing voice and brown eyes. There, on the air, in midafternoon, between Wayne Newton records, I would have a Lonely Name contest, with the winner getting a letter from me. Prudence Litwin is the loneliest name I have ever heard. She returned my letter unopened with *I do not accept mail from strangers* printed with excessive neatness just to the left of her own name on the envelope. No wonder she is so lonely.

Sometimes I go through the address part of the City Directory and pick out those strange addresses beside which, instead of a name, is listed only *Occupied.* And I wonder who those people are, so anonymous that they are not even included in that most impersonal of lists. I sympathize with their anonymity. There was a time when my address was a peach tree at the foot of a moun-

tain. Unfortunately, the Post Office showed a complete
lack of compassion, for I was eventually notified, by registered mail, that it was illegal to have a peach tree for an
address.

PRESERVING FIREWEED
FOR THE WHITE PASS
AND YUKON RAILROAD

"I really come from a town called Gene Autry, Oklahoma," says Gloria. "You know I wouldn't lie to you."

I'm inclined to believe Gloria. She has been up-front with me, ever since she moved into the room next to mine a month ago. After pulling weeds during the summer on the railroad right-of-ways around Whitehorse for the White Pass and Yukon Railroad, Gloria has settled into Vancouver for the winter. She draws Unemployment Insurance under one name, Welfare under two others, one in Vancouver, one in Burnaby. She has long, dark hair, over-sized brown eyes, an upturned nose, wears floor-length gingham dress, writes poetry, and carries a fat backpack the color of ripe blueberries.

"It wasn't always called Gene Autry," she goes on. "Back before I was born, the town—really it's only a general store and a Texaco gas pump— used to be called Foxx, Oklahoma. I think Foxx was a baseball player, but then he died, or retired, or was traded to a team nobody liked."

"How did you know what weeds to pull?" I ask. "What if you pulled up hundreds and hundreds of the Yukon National Flower?"

"They gave me a brochure," says Gloria. "It was full of

pictures of weeds. 'These are weeds,' the brochure said, 'and everything else isn't.' I could have been fired for pulling a weed that wasn't in the brochure. Ironically, fireweed is the flower of the Yukon," she adds.

"Did Gene Autry know he had a town named after him?"

"He must have—my dad said the story was in the *L.A. Times*. Old Simon Afraid-of-his-own-horses made a plaster statue of Gene Autry and his horse Champion. It stood out beside the highway for years; tourists used to stop and take pictures of it, and of the sign on the front of the general store. But the wind blew sand at the statue until all the paint was scoured off. People talked about repainting, but no one ever got around to it. A couple of years ago some kids tipped it over."

"I guess no one cares very much about Gene Autry anymore," I venture.

"Last spring the teacher asked the eighth-grade kids who Gene Autry was and not one knew."

"How soon they forget," I sigh.

It's been many long years since Gene Autry roped his last dogie; punched his last steer; stopped his last runaway buggy by leaping from the saddle to grab the bridles of the stampeding team; rescued his last breathless, redheaded heroine; sang his last song to that same red-headed schoolmarm, with a cardboard cactus and a silk-screened moon for a backdrop.

Champion is dead, sleeping in a cryogenic horse-trailer, swaddled in his favorite Navaho blanket, waiting for the resurrection.

Autry's California Angels baseball team struggles on, searching for the spectre of respectability which Autry has tried to buy with 14 million dollars. Autry, the white-hatted hero of a score of B-movies, should know that re-spectability is never for sale.

The town council of Gene Autry, Oklahoma has before it a notice of motion concerning a name change.

Simon Afraid-of-his-own-horses is building statues of Luke Skywalker and R2D2.

STRAWBERRY STEW

I have just spent an hour at the Public Library trying to find the technical name for the science of interpreting dreams, but I have failed. The cross-references are incestuous, and I haughtily ignore their tangle, which rubs about my ankles like a hungry cat. Should I find the right word now, by accident, I would not use it—I only wanted the name for a title. Since I cannot find what I want, I will call this piece something else, something exotic, something like Strawberry Stew.

Apparently, everyone dreams every night. I am seldom aware of my dreams. However, last night was an exception. I dreamt about a certain frigid prairie city where I spent my childhood. The time was the present, yet I stood on the outskirts of that city as it was thirty years ago, in a dismal area long-since cleared away for a housing development. My mother and my aunt, both dear ladies of impeccable character, who live in genteel retirement somewhere in Utah with a cat and a Bible, had apparently quarreled, and each had moved into one of the dilapidated houses which graced the area.

My aunt's house had about thirty rickety steps leading up to a side door. She stood at the top of those steps, mouthing unintelligible phrases and pointing incriminatingly at my mother, who stood some forty feet away on the veranda of her equally ramshackle house, pointing back.

While I was deciding on the best way to restore harmony between them, I discovered, in the overgrown yard between the houses, a flatbed truck, rusted and sinking into the ground, but with its cargo still intact. On the flatbed rested four jeeps, painted the curious camouflage brindle of the army, and well-preserved except for broken windshields and flat tires. I made my way through the tall grass, nettles, and raspberry canes to the front of the truck and found the date on the license plate to be 1944.

I put aside the problem of reuniting my mother and my aunt to consider how a flatbed truck full of jeeps could sit abandoned in someone's backyard for thirty years. As I studied the grey-green-brown patterns of the jeeps, I remembered how, as a child during the Second World War, I used to clip pictures of soldiers and military equipment from a comic strip in the *Star Weekly* called "Mandrake the Magician." I would line up the cut-outs in battle formations — gallant Allied soldiers on one side, horribly fanged Japanese on the other — and throw chunks of ice at them until one side was mutilated beyond recognition. The losers were invariably the Japanese.

The dream ended there.

Those of you who analyze dreams can perhaps supply me with an interpretation.

To atone in some small way for the propaganda-induced bias of my childhod war games, I think I will have supper tonight at a Japanese restaurant. I will, perhaps, inquire politely as to whether they serve Strawberry Stew.

ELECTRICO UTENSILIO

In Vancouver the Portuguese Mission is squeezed in between a fourth-rate Japanese restaurant and a newsstand patronized by middle-aged men in raincoats. It is about three blocks from the heart of the drag and because of that is not well attended. In Vancouver winos don't like to have to walk very far for their supper.

The night I went there I was their only customer. A lady in an expensive green dress ladled out some exquisitely seasoned soup with chunks of real meat in it. She had large, white, even teeth, and I surmised that she was married to a Portuguese dentist.

"Alimento," I said, making motions of stuffing my mouth with artichokes.

"Ah," said Señora Dentist, fussing about me in an international language. "Como se nombrar?"

"Electric Appliance," I responded.

"Señor U-ten-sil-i-o," she translated, dazzling me with her enamel smile.

An ambiguous little man stood behind a utility table watching me eat. He had a cantaloupe face and wore a tight white apron and a white cook's cap shaped like an overturned trough. As I ate my soup I composed his biography.

He had once been a cook for a group of Philippine insurgents. The rigors of battle led him to develop a severe addiction to rice wine. He more than once made soup from a Government soldier. The Portuguese lady found him hanging on a clothesline behind a tenement, sobered him up by reading a Philippine translation of the King James Bible, and when he was fully recovered made him first cook at this wino-less mission.

After I'd eaten, the dentist's lady ushered me into a tiny, cold chapel, presided over by a tiny, cold priest. He was made from black and white construction paper and flapped a little each time someone breathed.

"Señor Utensilio," she introduced me. The priest flapped gently.

"Gracias, gracias," I smiled and bowed backwardly into the kitchen area. As I left I took a tomato and a crusty roll from the utility table, and glared at the cook as though I had a row of medals on my chest and a service revolver pointed at his cannibal's heart.

THE BOOK BUYERS

The statistics are alarming. Television sets continue to multiply like evil cells in a jar, computers spew out information, while they propagate and proliferate like hamsters. People who live as slaves to the computer and television do not really need to know how to read; they move their lips and hold a finger under the line of copy they are reading, just like the average freshman university student—and sophomore, and junior. Seniors still move their lips, but they use their fingers to touch their genitals instead of underlining. None of the above-mentioned read books, unless it is the thin, large-print, full-of-pictures books on how to operate a computer.

Anyone aware of this situation would assume that reading is in its death throes. People communicate with cavemanlike grunts while watching car chases on their TV, their VCR, their computer, their word processor, and their blender. The car chase fly swatter and egg-turner is a hot item at 7-11 stores this month.

Yet, statistics state, and we all know that statistics never lie, that as a nation we are buying more books than ever before.

But since we are a nation of functional illiterates, who is reading all these books, you may well ask. Recently I decided to investigate.

I was in Toronto, and as we all know, there is nothing either west or east of Toronto. It seemed like a good place to start.

I visited a store called Longhouse Books, which sells only Canadian books. It is the only store in Toronto that sells Canadian books, for since it came into being the other 200 bookstores in Toronto no longer have to put up with the inconvenience of carrying anything printed in this country. The one person per week who inquires about a Canadian book is referred to Longhouse, while the other 200 stores fill their shelves with remaindered British novels, and picture biographies of "The Dukes of Hazzard."

I decided to find out who, in our state-of-the-art society, was actually buying all these books. I leaned against the Margaret Atwood wall at Longhouse; the wall was imported from a Central American country and had bullet holes, and blood stains, and "Yankee Go Home" written on it.

A young man in ankle-high construction boots, a parka and toque was shopping in the fiction section. He had a bottle opener and ski lift tickets attached to the zipper of his parka. His toque bore a crest reading "CBC Drinking Team." I knew I had stumbled on an average Canadian reader.

As I watched he bought *The Complete Works of Rudy Wiebe,* along with twelve volumes of Canadian poetry, each by an author whose last name began with H, as well as a critical book entitled *Hugh Maclennan and the Lost Continent of Atlantis, a Study of the Relationship Between the Ocean Floor and the Canadian Shield, as it Applies to Barometer Rising and Two Solitudes.*

The bill came to $102; he paid in crumpled bills which he pulled from several pockets. I noticed there were Molson Canadian caps mixed in with his change. With the books stacked in his arms he headed for the door.

"Pretty heavy reading," I said, holding the door open for him.

"Break your fucking back, eh, these goddamn books?"

"That wasn't exactly the connotation I had in mind."

"Eh?"

"Difficult reading?"

"I wouldn't know. If you're gonna flap your yap, Mac, you gotta carry some of this shit," and he thrust a bag of books into my arms.

"I presume you're traveling by subway?" I said, assuming my meaning would escape him. It did.

"Yeah, right after I deliver this shit. I gotta get home to Downsview, me and the old lady like to have a beer and watch "'Let's Make a Deal." The old lady gets her unemployment cheque today so she'll pick up a dozen Blue on the way home."

"Deliver?" I said, all ears.

"Yeah, I don't know what it's all about. But except for lugging all these books around it's an easy job. I usta work in a sawmill. I go to two stores a day, buy about a hundred dollars worth of books, and then deliver them to . . ." but he stopped, and a small gleam of suspicion shone through the murk of his eye.

"Guy who hired me, a Frenchy of some kind, said this was confidential stuff I was doin'. So you better not come no further with me."

He took back his sack of books and slogged off into the Yonge Street crowd.

The next day I leaned against the Pierre Berton wall at Longhouse; it was covered in white hair and money. I watched a woman buy over a hundred dollars worth of books, one of them was mine, so I knew she not only had good taste, but was probably literate as well, maybe even associated with a university. Something about her bothered me though, I guess it was because the lining of her coat dragged on the ground, maybe it was the three Eaton's shopping bags she carried jammed with old clothes and crumpled newspapers.

"I see you're a reader," I said as she left the store.

"Eh?"

"Ree-Der," I said, moving my lips.

"It's the communists who are doing it," she replied. "They open up the top of your head."

I noticed she was wearing what looked like a small antenna, made from the silver foil of cigarette packages. It was clipped into her gray hair by a small pink barrette in the shape of a puppy.

"You bought one of my books."

"I paid for them. They're my books. You buy your own. The NDP have kidnapped my grandchildren."

"You'll like my book. It attacks the bureaucracy. It's the one with the red and white cover."

"It's *my* book."

I stayed a half block behind her as she slopped down Yonge Street, cut through the Eaton's Center, stopping to berate a young man who stood in a doorway with a sign around his neck, offering his books for sale.

"You're in favor of abortion," she shouted at the young man, who looked mystified. "They'll burn your moustache off in hell."

Finally, she cut down an alley and into an unmarked door plated with sheet metal, at the back of a brick building. In about two minutes she emerged, stuffing money into the inside pockets of her coat.

I walked around the block. The building appeared vacant. There was plywood over the front windows. Above the door in pale letters was a sign: Enzio's Wholesale Hardware, Est. 1917.

I lurked in the alley for the rest of the day. Altogether eight people scuttled in and out of the doorway carrying bags of books from various bookstores. If eight people each spent $200 a day on books that would come to $1600 a day, $8,000 a week, $416,000 a year, in Toronto alone. What if there were phantom book buyers all across the country?

The next day I put ten of my own books into a Longhouse shopping bag and pushed open the sheet metal door. Inside there was a counter with a well-dressed young man behind it. Behind him were machines, clacking away, manufacturing something. What I supposed to be a foreman sat on a chair, monitoring a greenish computer.

The young man behind the counter had two computers at his disposal. When he looked up at me I tried to appear confused.

"I thought this was a used book store," I said.

He eyed me suspiciously.

"I saw people coming in with books and coming out with money. I brought you some books."

"You must be mistaken," said the man.

"No, there's the bag lady, the construction worker, the black man who goes around town saluting people . . ."

"We recycle wastepaper into cardboard cartons," the young man said, "but our supplies come from somewhere else . . ."

Just then the bag lady slopped through the door. She plopped a bag from Classic Books on the counter. "One hundred and ten dollars," she demanded, slapping down a receipt.

The young man smiled sickly.

"You're not a reporter?" he said to me, looking frightened.

"Not me," I said. "I'm a writer. This lady bought one of my books yesterday."

"We do buy books from a selected clientele," he said. "I note the titles in my computer here, drop them into a shredder and they're recycled into packing cases for computers, vcrs, word processors and the like."

"Sounds like a good job," I said, nodding toward the bag lady. "Where do I apply?"

"Canada Manpower," he said.

"Who funds the program?" I asked.

"I don't know if I should tell you this or not, but I believe it's the Prestige Agency of the Department of Economic Affairs."

"Prestige Agency?"

"It doesn't get much publicity," he said. "You see they realized years ago that by 1975 the book business would be dead, reading books would go the way of chautauquas, buggy whips, and mustache wax . . ."

"So, like all government programs, they decided to cover up the problem rather than treat it?" I said, grinning.

"That's universal government policy," he said. "You won't tell anyone about this?"

"Trust me. I assume there are other plants like this?"

"Dozens," he replied. "One in every large city, sub-

agents in every place that has a bookstore."

"Then if it wasn't for you the whole publishing business would be dead, the bookstores out of business, the authors more unemployed than usual?"

"True."

"There's a price for keeping quiet," I said. He looked at me apprehensively. "Every order from now on everywhere in the country has to include at least one of my books." I opened the sack I had been carrying and spread my books out on the counter. "I have nine books in all."

"I don't know," he said, eyeing a title, moving his lips as he read. "Your name is pretty long and hard to spell."

"Otherwise I'll go to the *Globe and Mail*."

"No one reads newspapers anymore either," he said, and smiled malevolently. "We send these same people out with rolls of quarters every morning to buy newspapers too. If it weren't for us the newspapers would have all been broke by 1978."

"I have friends at the CBC," I bluffed. "If this were to make it to *The Journal* it would ruin the economy. Can you imagine how gleefully Barbara Frum would report the news? How would you like to have this place full of TV cameras, the room crawling with reporters in mink coats and long dresses . . . and those are just the male reporters?"

"I see your point," he said. "I'll take it up with the Minister."

"I assume you don't write memos?" I said, but the implication eluded him.

So, the next time you buy a computer or a VCR, be kind to the box it came in, eh! That lovely, thick, corrugated cardboard is the essence of Canadian Literature.

Part Five

The Alligator Report

DOVES AND PROVERBS

If you wait on the bank of any river long enough
the body of your enemy will float by.
— Chinese Proverb

My friend Frankie should not drink. Because, when he in-
gests alcohol he turns into a dove. Other men, when they
drink, grow boisterous, sullen, or imagine themselves to
be Sugar Ray Leonard. Some, after a few drinks, become
great lovers. Frankie becomes a dove. The sad truth is
that a dove is only a glorified pigeon. It would take the
Birdman of Alcatraz and Peter, Paul and Mary, to distin-
guish a dove from a pigeon.

You cannot get a three-base hit by swinging a
banana.
— Biblical Proverb

Synthesizing himself into a 160-lb. dove is Frankie's
business. I mean, I have some idiosyncracies too. However, it is when Frankie develops the peaceful disposition
of a dove that the trouble starts. Would that he instead
developed little black fists and a winning smile.

A wet bird never flies at night.
— A Comedic Proverb

We are at a cocktail party.

"Hello," coos Frankie.

I notice that his spur is sticking out the back of his ox-ford. He is wearing shorts that may well be made of feathers. His legs are the color and consistency of yellow floor tile, and about as thick as a pencil. As Frankie takes another swallow of gin his purplish-gray feathers grow before my very eyes. *His* eyes are now orange. His beak is tan.

> The Chicago Cubs will win the last pennant before Armageddon.
> — A Milwaukee Proverb

Like Gilbert and Sullivan, I keep a little list of those who won't be missed. Frankie is accompanied by one of those near the top of my list.

> People who think they know everything sure piss off those of us who do.
> — A Romanian Proverb

"I've decided you guys should be friends," whooshes Frankie, his wing nestled around a cocktail glass. My enemy hulks beside Frankie, shaggy as a timber wolf. In Alberta, timber wolves often grow to a height of six feet, and, if they wear contact lenses, are allowed to teach in community colleges, though not in high schools.

"Rowl," says my enemy.

> Sheep have short memories.
> — The Politician's Proverb

Frankie attempts to flash the peace sign with his feath-
ered fingers. I can tell Frankie is still struggling, but he is
losing the battle with his uncontrollable desire to make
peace. Frankie's beak turns from tan to yellow; his
feathers sprout so rapidly I might be watching a time-
lapse camera.

> I was only taking my girlfriend for a drive in the
> country.
> —Charles Starkweather's Proverb

"You have so many common interests, you shouldn't
be enemies," says Frankie, though I'm sure I am the only
one who can understand him. To anyone else it sounds as
if Frankie is saying, "Coo, cooo, trrrrr, trrrr,
coooooooo."

My enemy stares at me through bloodshot contact
lenses. He teaches a seminar on *elastic* at a progressive
community college. We have about as much in common
as Mother Teresa and Idi Amin.

"Rowl," says my enemy, shrugging Frankie's wing off
his hairy shoulder.

> In Texas it is illegal to carry concealed wirecutters,
> or for a bachelor to own sheep.
> —The Rio Grande Proverb

"Blessed are the peacemakers, for they shall become
late-evening snacks," I say to my enemy. A small glint of
primordial intelligence appears in his eyes. Salivating, he
turns his long, hairy jaw toward Frankie, whose meta-
morphosis is now complete. He is a 160-lb. pigeon.

A foul ball hit behind third base is the short stop's
play.

—Proverbs 2-27

"Those who never attempt the absurd never achieve the impossible," coos Frankie. I am the only one who understands him.

My enemy has a mouthful of feathers.

The aim of literature is to create a strange object
covered with fur, which breaks your heart.
—Donald Barthelme's Proverb

"Rowl," says my enemy, feathers, like snowflakes, drifting in the air.

I AM AIRPORT

"Happy anniversary."

"For me? How thoughtful! Why it's . . . it's . . . a cigarette vending machine."

"Yeah. Well, I thought you'd be pleased. We're getting the urinal in the Red Concourse men's room fixed too."

"A vending machine for God's sake!" said the airport, and flounced out of the room.

It was, so to speak, the vending machine that broke the airport's back. Phantom pamphlets from Feminist News Service began appearing in departure lounges. The entire terminal trembled emotionally for 45 seconds the day Germaine Greer changed planes on her way to Tulsa. The tremble registered 4.2 on the Richter Scale.

An anonymous caller placed an ad in the daily newspaper.

The world would be a better place if more people loved their airports, it read. *How long since you've taken your airport dancing?* read another.

"The paint's peeling on your control tower. The down escalators aren't working. The newsstand's getting fat. The scrambled egg substitute in the cafeteria tastes exactly like the paper plates."

"So sue me," said the airport. She was wearing a chenille housecoat and smoking a cigarette.

"I think you're doing some of these things on purpose. Shape up!"

That afternoon, although it was only July, runway eight suffered frost-heave in three places.

The airport took to sighing every time a plane landed.

"Why is the airport unhappy, Mummy?" a child with golden curls asked her mother, who was dressed like a rodeo performer.

"Probably unfulfilled," replied the mother vaguely, twirling her lariat.

When was the last time you took your airport out to dinner without the kids along? Bring home a rose, perfume, or frilly underwear—or else, read the newspaper ads.

The management hired a topless cello player to entertain in the cocktail lounge.

Next morning, when the first maintenance men and sleepy-faced air traffic controllers arrived for work they found only an open field on which grazed an occasional brown cow, and a note which read: I can't stand being taken for granted any longer. Your socks are in the bottom drawer. There are TV dinners in the freezer. I am applying for a legal separation. I want custody of the youngest 707.

THE GERBIL THAT
ATE LOS ANGELES

It began by eating a hamlet in Vermont.

"Town's gone," one farmer said to another when they met on the spot that had once been the main street.

"Noticed it myself," said the other.

"Where you suppose it went?"

"Gerbil ate it, is what Maude Parker over at the telephone office says."

"Never known Maude to lie."

Routine missing hamlet reports were filed with the FBI. The gerbil moved grey across the land. It ate a village of four hundred in Blackhawk County, Iowa. Someone alerted the highway patrol. They said finding missing villages was not written into their union agreement. An enterprising ex-Bible salesman began selling bags of gerbil dung fertilizer to corn farmers.

There was a small commotion the morning that Kingsport, Tennessee, was missing. Several people who had relatives there threatened to write to their senators unless the relatives were returned. Johnny Cash and June Carter wrote a song called, "The Disappearance of Kingsport, Tennessee," and sang it at The Grand Ole Opry.

"It's dark this morning, " a man said to his wife as they walked down the front steps of their four-plex in Burbank.

"Smog," said the wife.

"Smells like the inside of a gerbil," the man, whose name was Tyrone, insisted.

"Instrument landings only," the controllers at Los Angeles International Airport told approaching aircraft.

A maintenance man found a sign lying in the middle of a runway. It read, "Welcome To Kingsport, Tennessee."

A Boeing 707, incoming from San Francisco, landed on what was supposedly runway seven, green concourse, only to touch down on fur. It came to a stop near the gerbil's right hip.

"Smells a little like burning gerbil hair," said the co-pilot, as the gerbil raised its right leg and scratched. The 707 was catapulted to a spot just west of Carson City, Nevada. The FAA called it an act of God.

The "Chatter" section of *People Magazine* asked, "What major west coast city is recently rumored to have been eaten by a gerbil?" They received only one reply, from a religious fanatic, who claimed he had predicted in 1964 that Los Angeles would be eaten by a gerbil, and offered to let *People* do a human interest story on him and his hobby of stuffing and mounting dahlias.

No one is admitting that anything unusual has happened.

The animal husbandry department of Kansas State University states unequivocally that it is impossible for a gerbil to swallow a city the size of Los Angeles.

Travel agencies are still booking tours to Disneyland.

"Nothing un-American has happened to Los Angeles," the President assured the nation last night.

The gerbil is said to be moving toward Seattle.

Stock in the Gerbil Dung Fertilizer Co., Inc. was up two points at yesterday's close.

THE HISTORY
OF PEANUT BUTTER

We know why the Mona Lisa smiles, what Napoleon was reaching for under his tunic, what was served at the Last Supper. Socrates drank from a cup of peanut butter. Charles Manson claimed it was an aphrodisiac. Charles Lindberg greased the propeller of the *Spirit of St. Louis* with it. If Amelia Earhart had not forgotten her peanut butter on the tarmac, she might still be flying.

I need not tell you what "Eureka! I've found it!" refers to. Ben Franklin flew a peanut butter kite. Isaac Newton was struck on the head by an apple-sized gob of it. Cortez and Balboa carried peanut butter to the New World, where it garnished the turkey at the first Thanksgiving.

There are eleven references to peanut butter in the plays of Shakespeare: terrorize any wizened academic by asking him to name them.

Who comforted Anne Frank, Ann Boleyn, Caryl Chessman, and Charles Starkweather in their final hours? Who leapt with the bomb from the hatch of the *Enola Gay?* What was used to fill the heart-shaped pool after Jayne Mansfield died and Mickey Hargitay failed to keep up the mortgage payments?

Peanuts are not nuts at all, but peas. They are roasted, toasted, fried, broiled, pressed, crushed, waffled, bent, spindled, stapled, and mutilated to produce: soap, face powder, shaving cream, shampoo, paint, plastics, livestock feed, cork substitute, wallboard, abrasives, explosives, coffee, and ink.

Peanut butter is also used to reinforce panty hose. Andy Granatelli was once forced to admit to a federal combines investigator that the prime ingredient in STP was peanut butter. Peanut butter makes a reliable contraceptive. A car fueled by peanut butter got over eighty mpg in city driving; unfortunately, General Motors bought the patent in 1932 and the formula has been suppressed to this day.

George Washington Carver (1864–1943) is known as the father of peanut butter. The Ku Klux Clan once burned a peanut butter cross on his lawn. In some countries, the Eucharist is celebrated with peanut butter instead of wine.

Peanuts grow below the ground; their plant has yellow flowers; the gestation period for peanuts is 120–140 days. Large litters are not uncommon. Peanuts make gentle and creative pets. Seymour and Vivian are nice names for your peanuts.

Biblical allusions are too numerous to catalogue. Shadrach, Meshach, and Abednego roasted peanuts in the fiery furnace. Daniel removed a peanut from the lion's paw. Biblical scholars have proven conclusively that Jesus did not walk upon water but upon floating peanut shells. Picture Ruth and Naomi, if you will, among the alien peanuts.

What is Behind the Green Door? What did Edgar Cayce know about peanuts that we don't? Garner Ted Armstrong is planning a special issue of *The Plain Truth,* dedicated to the power and glory of the peanut. The tablets that Joseph Smith brought down from the mountain

were really made of petrified peanut butter. What is the
secret ingredient in Coca Cola? What did Popeye really
eat?

Idi Amin is living in New Jersey, disguised as Mr. Peanut.

It is rumored that playing with peanut butter will
grow hair on the palms of your hands.

Elvis Presley was addicted to peanut butter pills. Janis
Joplin and Jim Hendrix OD'd on peanut butter. Barney
Clark received the first peanut butter transplant in 1982.

Finally, the 1934 movie, *Peanut Butter Madness,* shows
how nice, clean-cut teenagers turn into screaming, perverted sex-fiends after smoking as little as one gram of
peanut butter.

THE ALLIGATOR REPORT—
WITH QUESTIONS FOR
DISCUSSION

A water-laden wind blows from the ocean over the Everglades. An unlucky black-tipped ibis slams into a palm tree, drops to the sand like a five-pound plastic bag full of liver, lies quivering, the wind furrowing its feathers.

DO YOU SEE ANY SIGNIFICANCE IN THE DEAD BIRD
BEING AN IBIS? LOOK FOR REFERENCES TO THE IBIS
IN EGYPTIAN MYTHOLOGY. WOULD THIS PASSAGE
HAVE BEEN AS EFFECTIVE IF THE BIRD WERE AN
EGRET, HERON, FLAMINGO, OR ROSEATE SPOON-
BILL?

"Stay tuned to WTWT-TV," says Alvin Lee Wade, the anchorman, giving his audience a jowly, nearsighted smile. According to the latest ratings, Alvin Lee Wade smiles nearsightedly into 114,000 homes, bars, and motels in Talabogie County, Florida. "Right after this commercial break, we'll be back and have Buzz Hinkman with the sports, our own Charles Caulfield with the weather, and Carleen Treble with the Alligator Report."

WHY DO YOU THINK THE AUTHOR HAS CHOSEN TO
REPEAT HALF THE TITLE SO EARLY IN THE STORY?

SINCE NAMES ARE OFTEN AN IMPORTANT COMPO-
NENT OF A STORY, DO YOU SEE (SINCE THIS STORY IS
SET IN THE SOUTH) ANY SIGNIFICANCE IN THE AN-
CHORMAN'S SECOND NAME BEING LEE? WHAT
OTHER FAMOUS FICTIONAL CHARACER IS NAMED
CAULFIELD?

Preacher Gore watches Alvin's red cheeks and alcoholic nose fade away into a used car commercial. Outside his apartment, the wind blows high and a broken shutter chatters against the siding. Preacher is not an avocation but a Christian name, though he is not often called Preacher. Before his accident, he was known as Foot-to-the-Floor Gore, when he drove in local demolition derbies, dirt-track stock car races, and even once at Daytona Speedway.

WHY DO YOU THINK THE AUTHOR CHOOSES TO USE
THE WORD PREACHER TWICE, AND THE WORD
CHRISTIAN ONCE IN SENTENCE THREE? THE WORD
GORE HAS A NUMBER OF MEANINGS, ONE BEING "AN
ANGULAR POINT OF LAND." SINCE FLORIDA IS AN
ANGULAR POINT OF LAND, COULD THE NAME HAVE
SOME SIGNIFICANCE?

While waiting to go on the air, Carleen Treble is munching sensuously on the tail of a two-foot chocolate alligator which was delivered to her anonymously at the front desk that very afternoon. She thinks of it as an anonymous gift, though she knows it is from Preacher Gore. Preacher Gore is in love with Carleen Treble and in the past few months has gifted her with: twenty-four varieties of candy (culminating with the chocolate alligator), a pink princess phone, a gold fish, a doberman puppy, a tape deck for her car, a poster reading "Exonerate Shoeless Joe Jackson," a chrome cat with a clock in its belly, a pair of ice skates, a moped, a steamer trunk, a case of Saran Wrap, twelve pounds of pork chops, a microwave cooking course, a model kit of the Hindenburg, a case of Lipton's Chicken Noodle Soup, a Star Wars jigsaw puzzle, a cribbage board, his extra crutch, eight Willie Nelson records which he bought at a store owned by Burt Reynolds, and an alligator bowling ball bag which he made at physical therapy class. The doctors are worried that Preacher takes an inordinate amount of pleasure in making anything from alligator hide.

Although he didn't sign it, Preacher Gore left a note with the chocolate alligator. "If I'd listened to you," it said, "I'd be driving at Daytona, probably even in the Indy 500. I was watching the alligator report and I heard you plain as day say, 'There's alligators on the loose out around Old Sewanee Road and the Talabogie Swamp area. Now all you good ole boys be careful you don't get your Dingos bit,' and you smiled into that camera fit to break my heart."

THE CHOCOLATE ALLIGATOR IS SYMBOL OF SOMETHING. CAN YOU GUESS WHAT? SINCE ALLIGATORS USUALLY EAT PEOPLE, RATHER THAN PEOPLE EATING ALLIGATORS, CAN CARLEEN'S ACTION BE SEEN AS SIGNIFICANT? WHO WAS SHOELESS JOE JACKSON AND FROM WHAT SHOULD HE BE EXONERATED? CAN PREACHER'S NOTE BE INTERPRETED IN ANY WAY AS A PARABLE? SINCE WILLIE NELSON IS AN OUTLAW,

"Thus far, Hurricane Zoltan has dumped over four inches of rain on Talabogie County, and at last report the wind was blowing at 80 mph, or 125 kph, whichever is greater," says Charlie Caulfield, the weatherman, who for some reason is wearing a clown's red nose clipped over his own, and a scarlet jacket with a small white alligator on the pocket. The alligator is the symbol, mascot, and logo of WTWT-TV, *The Eyes of Talabogie County.*

SHOULD A HURRICANE EVER BE NAMED AFTER A MAN? OR IS THIS JUST A PLOY OF THE LIBERAL, COMMUNIST, DEMOCRAT, FEMINIST ALLIANCE TO DESTROY ALL THAT AMERICA STANDS FOR? AH HA! 125 KILOMETERS PER HOUR! ONLY COMMUNIST COUNTRIES USE KILOMETERS, METRES, AND UN-AMERICAN MEASUREMENTS LIKE THAT! NAME THREE OTHER SUREFIRE WAYS A CONCERNED AMERICAN CAN SPOT A COMMUNIST.

After another commercial for Mangrove Motors, and a promo for the Miss Teenage Talabogie County Contest—following a trumpet fanfare, the camera moves in on Carleen Treble. Carleen, as always, is dressed like a cheerleader, with knee-high white leather boots, a microskirt of red velvet, and a skimpy velvet halter with one breast red and one breast white, the red one having a white alligator embossed on it, the white one boasting a red alligator. As always, Carleen stands at attention as if somewhere in the back of her rather small mind the Star-Spangled Banner is waving in a gentle breeze. Carleen stares straight at her cue cards, or cute cards as she calls them, smiling vacantly, her grapefruit-colored hair cascading over her bare shoulders. She has a tiny smear of chocolate in the corner of her mouth. Carleen's hazel eyes move from side to side as she reads the Alligator Report. Her voice is untrained and whining but no one seems to notice—WTWT-TV's ratings have shown a steady upward movement since the Alligator Report began.

Right now, in Tampa, the executives of a much larger station are preparing a six-figure contract in an attempt to lure Carleen away from WTWT-TV.

"We've had six sightings in the last twenty-four hours," reads Carleen, "and our $30 award for the Alligator Sighting of the Day goes to Mrs. J. D. Commings, of Bobwhite Road, in Talabogie, for getting right on the Alligator Line, 282-4117, out-of-county call collect, and reporting that an eight-foot-long gator et her dog, Hannibal. 'Jest chomped him right in half,' Mrs. Commings said. So y'all watch for your $30 in the mail, Mrs. Commings. Maybe you can buy yourself a new doggie."

DO YOU THINK THE AUTHOR IS TRYING TO COMPEN-
SATE FOR THE COMMUNIST PROPAGANDA OF THE
PREVIOUS PARAGRAPHS BY MENTIONING THE STAR-
SPANGLED BANNER? SINCE GRAPEFRUIT IS A MAJOR
PRODUCT OF FLORIDA, COULD THE COLOR OF CAR-
LEEN'S HAIR IN ANY WAY BE A TOURIST PROMO-
TION? IS IT SIGNIFICANT THAT DOG SPELLED BACK-
WARDS IS GOD AND VICE VERSA? WHO WAS HANNI-
BAL AND WHY DID HE CROSS THE ALPS? DO YOU

THINK MRS. COMMINGS' DOG WAS NAMED AFTER 119
THE CARTHAGINIAN GENERAL OR THE CITY IN MIS-
SOURI? WRITE A 500-WORD ESSAY JUSTIFYING YOUR
CHOICE. SINCE MARK TWAIN THE FAMOUS HUMOR-
IST AND DOG-HATER HAILS FROM HANNIBAL, MIS-
SOURI, COULD THIS BE WHY THE AUTHOR ALLOWS
MRS. COMMINGS' DOG TO MEET SUCH A HORRIBLE
DEATH?

"Oh, Carleen, if I'd listened to you instead of letting
Lester Griff talk me into going hunting in the Talabogie
Swamp, I'd still have my right foot and still be driving
professionally, probably in the Indy 500," says Preacher
Gore, formerly known as Foot-to-the Floor Gore or just
plain Foot to his friends. Preacher is speaking to the sizzl-
ing black and white TV set in his apartment. He notes the
smear of chocolate in the corner of Carleen's mouth, and
hope springs eternal in his bruised and battered breast, for
Foot has lately had an encounter with the enemy. But in
his passion, a passion so complete that he can picture Carleen in her white boots standing at greasy stove cooking
up his favorite chile and clam casserole, he decides to ignore the enemy and buy Carleen a foot-long vibrator with
red eyes and a lolling tongue which he saw at *Kinks and
Things,* and have it delivered to her at WTWT-TV, anonymously of course.

After the accident, his right foot (Adidas, sock and all)
on the inside of a twelve-foot gator somewhere at the bottom of Talabogie Swamp, Preacher Gore had written to
Carleen Treble to thank her for the warning he had disre-
garded and to tell her how sweet her smile was. Carleen
read the letter over the air, then along with a camera

crew, went to visit the one-footed ex-stockcar driver at Talabogie County's City of Saviours Hospital: 22 stories, 626 rooms, the most modern equipment in all America, built as the result of a vision by Delbert Staggers, the blind giant.

Staggers, six feet nine inches, 330 lbs., slow moving, slow witted, his white eyes hidden behind blueberry tinted, mirrored sunglasses, was formerly employed by The Mob as a collector of bad debts. He was driven to the scene of his assignments by Pico the Rat, the 98-lb. cousin of the presiding warlord. Pico would point out the debtor and guide Delbert Staggers forward until contact was made. Delbert would whack the debtor unmercifully with his white cane until he either paid up or fainted. He spent his days pummeling myopic Spanish fruit stand owners, and losers in shiny suits with stained fingers and ties who had blown their welfare cheques at the dog tracks.

Then, one afternoon when there were no collections to be made, Pico the Rat took Delbert Staggers to see *Rocky*. Delbert could only hear the movie. But he cheered Rocky in his final battle for the championship and several times shouted, "I'll loan ya my cane, Rocky! I'll loan ya my cane."

WRITE A COHERENT PARAGRAPH DEMONSTRATING THE OBVIOUS RELATIONSHIP BETWEEN THE FACT THAT DELBERT STAGGERS CARRIES A CANE AND THE CORRECT ANSWER TO THE RIDDLE OF THE SPHINX, MAN.

Behind his blueberry glasses Delbert had a vision. "If

Rocky can fight for the heavyweight championship, then
I can build a hospital." He reached over and put his large,
red hand on Pico's birdlike arm. "Give me a hundred
dollars or I'll give you a compound fracture," he said to
Pico. And the rest is history.

The City of Saviours Hospital emerged from the Everglades, just off a secondary highway, a mile inside the
Talabogie County line. At Delbert's instruction, Pico the
Rat had a logo prepared showing Christ's head erupting
in a blaze of heavenly light from the top of a 22-story
building. The stationery on which the logo appeared was
thick and cream colored. Pico used his connections with
The Mob to obtain the mailing lists of several TV evangel-
ists and sent out 222,000 letters with Delbert Staggers'
signature, demanding money for the City of Saviours
project and suggesting that a certain vaguely defined
plague would befall those who didn't contribute gener-
ously.

When the money began rolling in, Pico established, on
paper only, his own medical supply wholesale firm,
through which all equipment for City of Saviours passed,
marked up 222%, a number which Pico considered lucky.

Only one minor problem surfaced. Talabogie County
already had two major hopsitals and was in no need of a
third. Soon, City of Saviours boasted a staff of over
5,000—all hired through the P.R. Personnel Agency,
president, Pico the Rat, which claimed six months' salary
as its reward for placing the right person in the right job.

Only in the case of natural disasters like Hurricane Zoltan, or if someone like Preacher Gore was unlucky
enough to get his foot bitten off in the immediate area of
the hospital, did it ever operate at even 10% of capacity.

The staff held daily Scrabble tournaments and the doctors played polo and miniature golf on the landscaped grounds. For rainy days, there were the five bowling alleys in the maternity wing.

After she and the camera crew visited Preacher Gore at City of Saviours, Carleen Treble was taken on a tour of the hospital and introduced to Delbert Staggers, who sat behind a wide chrome desk topped with blueberry tinted glass. Although blind from birth, Delbert Staggers imagined he looked like Elvis Presley.

"Oh, Mr. Staggers, or should I say Reverend Staggers, I just love your blue glasses. I look so good reflected in them," said Carleen.

"I want you, I need you, I love you," said Delbert.

IN DESCRIBING DELBERT STAGGERS, DO YOU THINK THE AUTHOR WAS FAMILIAR WITH THE FOLLOWING BIBLICAL QUOTATION: "THERE WERE GIANTS IN THE EARTH," GEN. 6:4? NOTE HOW BLUEBERRIES ARE ASSOCIATED WITH STAGGERS. DID YOU KNOW THAT ALL BLUEBERRIES HAVE TEN — AND ONLY TEN — SEEDS? DO YOU THINK THAT HAS ANYTHING TO DO WITH *this* STORY? THERE IS A NERVOUS DISEASE OF HORSES AND CATTLE CALLED *blind staggers:* CONSULT A VETERINARIAN AND LEARN THE SYMPTOMS. HOW DO THEY APPLY TO DELBERT AND PICO? IF YOU DON'T ALREADY OWN ONE, ASK SOMEONE CLOSE TO YOU TO BUY YOU A HORSE.

Carleen Treble and Delbert Staggers immediately became an item, as it were. And while Foot Gore, the alligator-bitten, lovesick, ex-stockcar driver showered Carleen with his dubious gifts, she was spending six night a week and Sundays after church with Delbert Staggers.

Pico the Rat often got to open the envelopes full of $100 bills which poured in every day in response to the vaguely threatening letters of Delbert Staggers—letters that intimated he was a minister of the gospel. Pico knew a good thing when he was onto one, and ordered for Delbert, by mail, several doctoral degrees ranging in scope from Divinity to Zoology, all of which subsequently appeared on the letterhead and under Delbert's signature. As the letters became more threatening, the response from the lunatic fringe of Christianity to whom they were directed increased in direct proportion to the nastiness of the request.

Delbert knew nothing about the changing tone of his letters or the acquisition of degrees. He was only interested in Carleen. He had made the earthshaking discovery that sex did not require 20/20 vision, and rested easy in his excesses, confident that overdosing was unlikely to damage his eyesight. Carleen loved it when he quoted from Elvis Presley, and made Delbert leave his blue glasses on while they made love so she could practice her various expressions of passion. For Carleen had no intention of always delivering the Alligator Report for WTWT-TV, but harbored ambitions of acting, singing gospel music, and being elected to the state senate.

When Pico the Rat found out about Foot sending presents to Carleen he immediately got on the phone.

"Listen, Foot," he said, trying to sound like 98 lbs. of menace, "it would be very unhealthy for you to keep on sending unsolicited presents to a certain female TV personality."

"So what are you gonna do, send another alligator to bite off my other foot?" said Foot.

"Live in fear," said Pico the Rat, and hung up.

Foot Gore went out and bought a $200 gilt frame, inserted a photograph of his mother into it, and mailed it special delivery to Carleen Treble.

NOTE HOW A MAN NAMED FOOT LOSES A FOOT TO AN ALLIGATOR. IF YOU ARE NOT FAMILIAR WITH THE STORY OF OEDIPUS, ASK YOUR INSTRUCTOR TO TELL IT TO YOU. WHY DO YOU THINK FOOT MAILS A PICTURE OF HIS MOTHER TO CARLEEN? COULD IT BE THAT HE SUFFERS FROM AN OEDIPUS COMPLEX? OEDIPUS PUTS OUT HIS EYES. DELBERT STAGGERS IS BLIND. COULD IT BE THAT FOOT AND DELBERT ARE DIFFERENT SIDES OF THE SAME PERSONALITY? WHERE DOES THAT LEAVE CARLEEN? IS ELVIS PRESLEY REALLY DEAD?

The next afternoon, a Cadillac limousine pulled up in front of Foot's apartment and a weasel-faced runt in an oversized chauffeur's uniform guided a giant wearing mirrored sunglasses toward the door. When Foot answered the bell, he was first pushed back into the apartment by a poke in the belly, then struck sharply across the ribs by Delbert's white cane. Inside the apartment, Delbert whacked him into unconsciousness.

"Wait outside. I'll collect the money," said Pico.

"I've forgotten more than you'll ever know," Delbert said to Foot. Delbert thought he was punishing an ex-employee who had embezzled funds from the hospital.

"Stop annoying Carleen Treble or next time I *will*

bring an alligator," hissed Pico into Foot's semi-conscious
ear.

Today, the Alligator Report over, Carleen's vacuous smile fading into a feminine hygiene commercial, Preacher switches off the set, dons a yellow slicker, and exits, leaning into the bitter wind of Hurricane Zoltan. He stumps along the beach on his cork, balsa-wood, and styrofoam prosthetic.

A half mile up the beach he spots the dead ibis on the sand beneath a palm tree. He picks it up, examines it, decides (ignoring the pain in his ribs) that he will send it by special delivery parcel to Carleen at the TV station.

IS IT LEGAL TO POST A DEAD IBIS IN THE U.S. MAIL?
SUGGEST TO YOUR PRINCIPAL THAT HE ORGANIZE A
FIELD TRIP TO THE NEAREST POST OFFICE.

The ibis has drawn one leg up into its feathers. Foot Gore carries it by the other leg, swinging it in time as he whistles the march from *The Bridge on the River Kwai.* Disguised as wild orchids, two postal inspectors follow at a discreet distance.

HOW SIGNIFICANT IS THE IBIS APPEARING TO HAVE
ONLY ONE LEG? COULD THE AUTHOR BE REFERRING
TO THE FOOTLESS BIRD LEGEND? READ THE COM-
PLETE WORKS OF D. H. LAWRENCE AND TENNESSEE
WILLIAMS TO FIND OUT.

The wind whips sand against Foot-to-the-Floor Gore's pant legs. As he walks, he pictures Carleen opening the box and finding the ibis. He wiggles the toes on his right foot. He can feel the sand collecting in his artificial shoe.